FOUR TAKEAWAYS AND A FUNERAL

Book 3 Bellydancing and Beyond Series

KERRIE NOOR

CONTENTS

MEET THE GANG

Some Of The Ol' Characters From Downfall Of A Bellydancer.

Nefertiti: she who must be heard and narrates Mavis's story in her own unique style.

Mavis: Lochgilphead's postmistress; a woman who can add, subtract, and lick a stamp all at the same time and while holding a conversation.

Lumpy: the janitor in the community centre. His toolbox is legendary.

Sheryl: The inspiration for Mavis's wedding plans.

Steven: the sort of man no one noticed, until he married Sheryl.

Rodger: the *ex*-love of Nefertiti's life.

Shifty: the owner of the Argyll, who liked to think his pub more than just a local boozer, and Rodger's new partner.

Puss: Nefertiti's cat, who likes to think she belongs to the Bag Lady.

The Bag Lady: Formerly known as the Co-op Bag Lady, from a time when she sat in front of the co-op playing her organ. Now camped in Nefertiti's garden, she plays the drum and feeds Puss, despite what Nefertiti says.

Betty: Shifty's mother and the Bag Lady's partner in crime.

Bingo: Shifty's dog; famous for attacking Nefertiti's glitter bra during her performance at the old folks' do in the Argyll, the only reason Rodger puts up with him. Legend has it Bingo still has the bra, which he lugs around like a security blanket.

New Additions

Tenzam: works in the Taj; so good at his job he bought his mother a seventy-five-inch TV from his tips alone.

Fanny: Mavis's sister, a healer who saves lives with emergency massages and herbal tablets.

The Roadworks Man: a man who, despite spending most of his time filling potholes in roads, knows everything about everything.

Amanda: the new owner of the bookshop; a believer in stories, paper books, and real coffee.

The Rod Man: great pals with the Roadworks Man; they have been known to argue over the conditions of the roads and what a real bhuna should taste like. Nothing remains blocked when he is around—his rods are legendary.

Cat: Mavis's mum; the sort of mother that played with her makeup rather than her children.

Bit Parts

Jessie: a woman who wants to please her parents but knows in her heart it will never happen.

Birthday Dad: Jessie's dad.

The Wife: Jessie's mum.

Kamal: the chef in Ban Duic, the sister restaurant to the Taj; an Asian man with a Glasgow accent. Has confused more than a few drunks.

Very Bit Parts

Heather: Cat's favourite carer.

Mrs Campbell: a destructive woman with no control over her mouth.

Madge: an elderly woman who uses her Zimmer frame to queue-jump.

Charlie: a chirpy boy who uses his wheelchair to run over the toes of people he doesn't like.

GLOSSARY

Whip-Around: a collection for someone less fortunate than those organising the said "whip-around." No charities' or paperwork are involved.

Scraps: deep-fried batter that is left over in the fryer from frying fish. Some fight over the delicacy, others throw it to the birds, and most curse the stuff when it blocks up the sink.

The tick: "buy now, pay later"; very popular before credit cards.

Chippie: a fish-and-chip shop famous for giving away scraps, wanted or not.

Strictly: short for *Strictly Come Dancing*, a Saturday-night TV show that has replaced going out and makes a takeaway taste that bit better.

Shag: once known as a name for a large pelican-like bird, now more known as the type of sex after one to many in the pub or when there is nothing on the telly but *Strictly* repeats.

Nippy: the sort of niggly feeling a woman gets when TV, takeaway, or a shag doesn't live up to expectation. Sometimes induced by excessively long queues at the co-op.

Sloe gin: berry soaked in gin. The only thing slow about it is pricking the berry before soaking them.

"Swanking," "swanked," or "to swank": a popular word used in the pantomime world; prancing, pranced, or to prance.

Joiner: makes much more sense than "carpenter" (which has nothing to do with carpets).

Taj Mahal: also known as "the Taj," a traditional name for "the Indian"; there is one in every Scottish town (well, almost).

"The Dog's Bollocks": not strictly a Scottish expression but more an old-fashioned English expression for "it's fantastic!" now replaced by "awesome!" Often shortened to "the dog's" but never "the bollocks." (Without the word "dogs" in front of the word "bollocks," "bollocks" reverts to the opposite meaning, e.g., "That's bollocks," "You're talking bollocks," or just "Bollocks.")

The Women's Guild and WRI: a dying breed of women who like to enter baking competitions and pray before meetings. They took the homemade scone, jam, and sponge to a level that has never been equalled by the co-op, Tesco's, or Marks & Spencer's.

Ol' Boy: Old man who usually has something to say and will say it whether anyone is listening or not.

Tenner: not strictly a Scottish term but a shortened version of ten pounds or dollars, usually used when asking for a loan: "Give us a tenner."

Scotch Pie: tough-as-boots pastry with unrecognisable meat that requires Heinz's baked beans poured on top to hide the taste.

The Deep Heat Joke: origins unknown. A phallic play on the words "Deep Heat," which is strong-smelling cream used for sore muscles. It is quickly absorbed, stains everything, and has lasting effects of a couple of minutes . . . if lucky.

The Down-Under Joke: similar to the Deep Heat joke but requires less imagination.

An Indian: the great British Tradition, usually with or after a few pints. It has a menu like a book with dishes impossible to pronounce or remember, hence people always order the same thing.

Curries are either . . .

Hot: naga, madras

Middle-of-the-Road (although some would argue hot): jalfrezi, Jaipuri

Impressive: balti; mixed grill, which comes sizzling on a hot plate held high above the head – for the show-off waiter

Mild: korma, pasanda

Dry: bhuna

Soups: dhal

Rice dishes: biriyani

Deep-fried bite-size treats: bhaji, pakora

And that is just a wee taster . . .

Roughcast: a common phrase. In Lochgilphead it is considered traditional to cover a new building with a grey-cement-and-pebble surface so rough you can, according to the Bag Lady, skin a potato with it.

"Oot & aboot": Scottish for "out and about," a term rarely used in the Highlands due to the weather.

Zimmer Frame: Named after Mr Zimmer, a man who spent his days walking around the supermarket wheeling an empty trolley. Now used by the elderly in Scotland as weapons of mass destruction for queue-jumping.

Hen: a term of affection for women in Scotland, unless when spoken by a farmer.

Bollocking & Ballistic: The two B words that are usually used when the loss of temper is far greater than the reason behind it.

"Flower of Scotland": A song the Scottish sing when they want to win . . . and will continue to sing even when they have lost.

Thingmies: Scottish for "thingies" – anything you can't remember the name of.

Travelling stock: also called "travelling folk"; people whose ancestors lived the life of a gypsy, who offered good luck if their "palms were crossed with silver" and often seemed to have a connection with dogs and horses.

Doing My Head In: that feeling you get when forced to listen to your neighbour's eighteen-year-old's music at 3am while trying to sleep.

Brae: Scottish term for "steep hill"; in Lochgilphead it is the steep walk up to the A&E or hospital for mental health problems. Hence the term "he's up the brae" usually means he's not only up the hill but in residence for a while.

Buckie or Buckfast: A traditional Scottish drink for those who can't afford vodka and Red Bull but are looking for the same effect.

Shinty: Scottish game for people with no fear.

Banoffee Pie: dessert made with bananas and cream which is not only delicious but one of your five-a-day.

The Kilt: a garment that liberates a man. Suddenly he is prancing about in public, swinging his hips in a "hide and seek" fashion about what's underneath. He will dance at weddings like something out of *Strictly Come Dancing* and walk like he has an arse worth looking at. The kilt holds a seductive promise, often with a larger-than-life sporran swaying in the front, suggesting something spectacular. And woman love it, even after whisky takes hold and flashing brings the mystery to a close. Women still love it!

To Cave In or Give In: Apparently (according to Beryl – or was it Mavis?) a hangover in the sun can do that to a man; something to do with testosterone at 35 degrees.

Midges: invisible insects that come out on a warm summer's evening to bite anyone on the west coast of Scotland. Apparently drinking whisky keeps them away.

Half Cut: another word for "three sheets to the wind"; inebriated, blootered, drunk.

Spin a Yarn: Storytelling while spinning wool. (I suspect this is Australian.)

Sticky Willow: sticky, green, vine-like plant that sticks like Velcro to your clothes.

Highland Fling: the fling of a Highland man, which has nothing to do with sex and everything to do with wearing a kilt and flinging it about the place while dancing.

A Do: an event that's worth getting your legs waxed for.

Al Fresco Dancing: dancing outside; no picnic or audience required.

"How's it hangin', hen?": a phrase that has nothing to do with hanging or hens, but is a Scottish way of sexing up a "How are you?"

Simmet: Scottish for "vest," usually the itchy variety worn by those who remember the War.

PROLOGUE

"Love at First Dip"

Mavis and Lumpy had decided to get married, and they planned a small do with a "hot and spicy" theme, a few close friends, and a celebrant on Skype.

"We want no fuss," said Mavis. "Just lots of food, great photos, and belly dancing."

Mavis and Lumpy have been an item for about a year – and a happy Mavis has taken a bit of getting used to. While I've spent the past year on my own, struggling with blocked drains and leaking roofs, Mavis has moved in with her soulmate – a man who loves to cook, occasionally cleans, and has even been seen stocking up on massage oils at the chemist.

Lumpy has turned out to be quite a catch. Not only is he comfortable with a hammer, he cooks like a pro – his latest passion being all things hot, spicy, and foreign. He can take mincemeat, mashed potatoes, and even toasted cheese to a new level of exotic, tongue-tantalising, "what the hell is burning my mouth?" treat. Nothing, according to Mavis, passes his lips without a hint of turmeric or a dash of ginger.

And Mavis, it seemed, was happy – until the Taj Mahal reopened.

The Taj Mahal is the only Indian restaurant for miles and had been closed for years One day, with no warning, the "Closed" sign was turned to "Open," and soon there was a queue on a Friday night. The pakoras are legendary. A police shift is never complete without a bag of them, and The Roadworks Man, who has practically lived at the place since it opened, swears by their aphrodisiac qualities. *Although I have yet to see any evidence.*

Lumpy took one bite of Tenzam's pakoras and stated that they were "the dog's bollocks."

At first, the chief took offence – until he saw Lumpy's review on TripAdvisor. Lumpy talked of pakoras like they were as elusive as truffles and as succulent as fillet steak...

"His chicken is as soft as butter, coated in batter that snaps, crackles, and pops. One bite and you'll never look at a battered sausage again. As for any vegans out there, the chief will rustle up a tofu that would fool a Texan."

What a Texan had to do with tofu I have no idea, but it rubbed the chief up the right way – so much so that Lumpy began to put on weight.

"Pakoras are the way to go," he was fond of saying. But Mavis, it seems, was beginning to suffer...

She was finishing up her shift at the post office when I walked in. Normally, she would want a coffee so we could talk about her wedding plans, but this time she looked frazzled. I made a joke about spice being more than just a mouthful, expecting a smart comment back, but what I got was a glum look.

Mavis pulled out a peppermint and began to crunch. "I had no idea that pleasing a man would involve so much... indigestion." She swallowed.

I thought I saw a tear in her eye, and I asked her what was wrong.

"Lumpy knows I'm a korma woman at heart," she huffed and pulled out a tissue. "I may occasionally venture into a jalfrezi, but this whole spice thing..." She dabbed at her nose. "...it's too much! I mean, green chilli and eggs for breakfast? How can anyone face that over breakfast TV?" She blew her nose.

"I see," I said.

She slammed the till shut. "Why should Lumpy always have what he wants?"

I was taken aback. I looked at Mavis. It wasn't that long ago she was saying the opposite − "Why shouldn't he have what he wants?" − and had even made jokes what she "did" for love.

"I laugh in the face of heartburn," she'd said. Mind you, she'd been at the Bag Lady's sloe gin at the time.

I stared at her wilted face. What had changed her?

"He spends more time with that chef than me... and the chef hardly speaks English. I mean, what have they got to talk about?" She slapped some coins into a bag and tossed them into the safe. "Every time I look for Lumpy, there he is in the takeaway, chomping into something extra large and triple fried. What's that doing to his heart?"

Mavis walked to the door, pulled the sign to "Closed," and stared at me. "And they are always watching some Bollywood film full of young women, half dressed and dancing in the rain. What's that doing to *my* heart?"

Lumpy had always been partial to dancing, but I didn't have the heart to remind her.

"I never see him anymore," she muttered.

"Maybe it's wedding nerves," I said with little conviction.

"Yes, well," she snorted. "Weddings are all about compromise, and now it seems he can't even spell the word!"

Chapter One

THE FISH SUPPER

We all want to believe in a happy ever after, even if it's someone else's.

Mavis wanted a wedding like Sheryl's, except for the secret bit. Mavis wanted everyone to know about her wedding, while Sheryl didn't tell a soul. In fact, it was only once Sheryl had blogged about her wedding that anyone knew—apart from me.

Mavis, on the other hand, was as public as a celebrity on *Big Brother*. Within minutes of Lumpy's proposal, she was on not only the phone but Facebook, Instagram, and Twitter, hashtagging selfies like a teenager.

She was so happy it was sickening.

"We have been together six months," tweeted Mavis. "Barely time to change the sheets and there he was, ring in one hand and bubbly in the other."

Lumpy had pushed the boat out with a ring the size of a bath plug, along with promises of a ceremony no one would forget...

The day Lumpy proposed, he said little; instead he spent the day with Mavis making his kitchen "their" kitchen and then "nipped out for a fish supper." Mavis had no idea about a ring.

Lumpy returned "all romantic and sheepish" with a cod and chips under one arm and a bottle of Prosecco in the other.

Mavis, engrossed in *The X Factor*, didn't notice until Lumpy, on one dodgy knee, handed her her cod.

"For you," he said. "A woman any good man would want."

Mavis was confused. "Cod?" she said. "I asked for haddock." Then, from behind his back, Lumpy pulled the ring. Mavis was swept off her feet.

Later that night, Mavis, tucked up in bed with the "man of her dreams," tweeted:

"Dinner's in the dog; who could look at batter after a proposal?"

In the months that followed, Mavis and Lumpy talked, discussed, and finally disagreed over the wedding; each had different ideas. Mavis saw a chandelier setting, an outfit that would be talked about for weeks, and a professionally made video.

"The sort of video," said Mavis, "that would even have my mother tearful – a woman who never cried at anything apart from a fistful of onions."

Lumpy on the other hand saw a cheap-as-chips venue, DIY decorations, and a mobile phone video knocked up by his good pal the Roadworks Man.

Neither of which was anything like Sheryl's wedding.

Sheryl and Steven were married on a beach a few miles from Campbeltown. The celebrant was a good pal of Sheryl's, while Steven's cousin and his wife were the witnesses.

The wife, known only as "the wife" due to her caustic nature, was tolerated by many because everyone felt for Campbell, the "gem of a husband" who "put up with so much."

Campbell, being a farmer, offered Steven half a sheep to celebrate. His wife, who came from the suburbs, said "a leg" and, before Steven could answer, changed the offer to "a shank with a few turnips thrown in." Steven, reading between the lines of a half-hearted offer, suggested cake and sandwiches, which he would bring.

Steven made Sheryl's favourite chocolate cake with cream icing. The cake was completely over the top, with three layers and a twirling belly dancer for each member of my now de-flunked troupe – mine being a likeness as much like me as co-op curry being like...a curry.

Sheryl was married in a lemon outfit that most people wouldn't be seen cleaning an oven in, let alone wear to a "do." Yet, somehow, it worked. Sheryl, voluptuous and sparkling, looked radiant in lemon dungarees, see-through blouse, and glitter-covered bra. While Steven, in a white shirt and a Kris Kristofferson beard, looked like he had won not only a watch but the factory it was made in.

Sheryl's *Married in Lemon* blog inspired people with a mixture of hope, romance, and "why not me?" feeling. But then Sheryl's blog always inspires. She blogs about wearing what you like, enjoying food, and how large is just a five-letter word.

Mavis took one look at the *Married in Lemon* blog and saw romance, an unusual setting, and a whole new colour scheme for her wedding.

"That's what I want," she said.

I thought she was joking. I mean, Mavis is not what you would call a beach person, and I couldn't see her in dungarees eating sandwiches.

Mavis's mother thought the same and launched into a spiel about dungarees not "suiting" a mature woman whose waist had "left years ago."

While Lumpy thought Mavis, like him, wanted marriage on a shoe-string. And, without asking, Mavis accepted a "too good to be true" offer from work.

Lumpy, after years of keeping the toilet to a standard high enough to "eat your lunch off" in the community centre, had been offered a room in the community centre along with free use of the kitchen with all the teabags at his disposal. Lumpy was over the moon, and when the after-school playgroup had offered to decorate, and the Woman's Guild make a "fab" cake, Lumpy was ecstatic.

"It will be fab," he said to Mavis...

Mavis thought he was joking. *Lumpy saying "fab" is as believable as Campbell's wife saying "help yourself."*

"Aye right," she said with a laugh, and then she saw his face.

Now disappointed and confused, Mavis is not sure what to do next. Lumpy told her he was going to give her "a day to remember."

Now it seems that it was going to be a day she would rather forget.

Chapter Two

SLOE GIN

One man's meat is another woman's cake.

After closing the post office, Mavis followed me home and proceeded to tuck into my sloe gin with relish. We were sitting by the Bag Lady's campfire with Sheryl, the Bag Lady, and her greatest pal, Betty. Mavis was on a downer and seemed to think that sloe gin was the answer, while Sheryl, also tucking into the sloe gin, talked about her wedding. Sheryl was trying to cheer Mavis up, although how she thought gloating about her wedding would help I have no idea.

With a glowing face and "Steven" in every sentence, Sheryl described what we had already heard. A two-day honeymoon in a one-berth caravan. Campbell had given them the use of his caravan at the back of one of his fields and, according to "the wife," they didn't emerge once. Even I found it a bit much, despite being heavy-handed with the gin.

"Steven had organised it all," said Sheryl.

"Hurrah for Steven," muttered Mavis.

"Two days on cake and bubbly," said Sheryl. She laughed. "It was the best."

"That's love for you," huffed Mavis, poking at the fire.

"We walked along the beach, staring at the sheep, and that's when it hit me."

"Please don't talk about vegetarianism again," said Betty. "Shifty's cooking steak." She sighed.

Shifty, Betty's son, periodically cooked her rare meat, usually after a row, and he was feeling guilty. Betty's slim legs had him worried about her bones and he believed all things red and bloody would build her up. Betty downed her drink as Sheryl continued to talk, then topped up everyone's glasses – except Sheryl's.

"A caravan?" I said to Mavis. "Is that what you want? A honeymoon in a tin can with a shower the size of a dog kennel, that rocks with every move..."

Sheryl glared at me.

"...surrounded by sheep droppings?"

"Essentially no," muttered Mavis. "Just, the spirit of it all – the romance; the intimacy..."

"In a caravan?" said the Bag Lady.

Sheryl glared at the Bag Lady.

"Well no..."

Mavis downed her drink. "Of course mum doesn't help, Lumpy can do no wrong in her eyes. She thinks a bring-your-own-bottle in the community centre is a great way to get hitched. I mean the playgroups met there – I'd be better off with sheep droppings."

"There weren't that many sheep droppings," muttered Sheryl.

Mavis looked at her empty glass. "Mum says I should be grateful for anything at my age."

"You're lucky," said Sheryl. "My mum sulked for days. I think she was annoyed she wasn't there. I told her that as it was on a beach, I would have had to build a ramp for her wheelchair. Then I would need to ask my sister to take her, *who'd ruin everything*. And then Steven would have to ask his family, *who'd ruin whatever my sister had missed*. Then we would have to accept Campbell's half a sheep, which would mean I would have to return some DIY favour to Campbell wife, who would completely milk it and I would be working my arse off for the next six months."

Sheryl looked from one face to another. "And where's the romance in all that?"

"Exactly," said Mavis.

"When I got married there was no one," said Betty. "It was so small we had it at McDonald's – a Big Mac followed by a McFlurry, and did I complain?"

No one took her seriously.

"No, because he was doing his best."

I poured another drink as Betty talked about a robust man who wore jeans like they were painted on and "swanked about the place." Apparently, women loved him. It was all to do with an unbuttoned shirt and chest hair. And, of course, nothing like the man she married…I'd seen the photos.

Betty stared at the fire and smiled to herself. "It was back in the seventies," she said, "when men were hairy and proud of it."

Mavis sighed. Usually she was the first in with a "you're talking through your arse" comment, but not this time. She looked at Sheryl.

"Lumpy says that he wished all women were like you."

I, missing the point completely and thinking Mavis was talking about Sheryl's outfit, told Mavis that yellow was not her colour.

Mavis called me superficial.

"You don't get the point," she said. "It's not about Sheryl's lemon, it's about agreeing. Lumpy thinks that Sheryl agrees with Steven all the time, and when I tell him it is only half the time because they compromise, he gets all uppity. 'Like I do with you,' he says." Mavis snorted. "As if!"

"One person's compromise is another's giving in," said the Bag Lady.

"I told him I wanted a fine dining experience," said Mavis. "He said fine dining was his idea of hell – not fun." Mavis looked at her fingers. "Apparently eating a curry with your hands is."

"Some say you get the true taste of a curry that way," said the Bag Lady.

Betty dribbled a smidgen of sloe gin in Mavis's glass.

"He's come up with this stupid idea of sitting on the floor eating curry. No presents, just joss sticks and scattered rose petals."

She tossed the twig into the fire with a weak smile. "His family thinks it's a great idea. Well, I told him," said Mavis, "Lumpy, I said, fun is a three-letter word, and there are two in a marriage."

We all looked at her.

"Lumpy then said, two meaning you and you—not me." She sighed. "...and that's when I called him pedantic."

Mavis sort of killed the evening after that.

The Bag Lady slipped into her tent with a curt zipping-up, while Sheryl with an "I give up" look called Steven for a lift.

I watched Mavis look as downcast as a sunset in the rain. She had been so excited when Lumpy proposed six months ago. Now she looked as miserable as the days before she discovered belly dancing.

Chapter Three

UNEMPLOYED

A beer in the hand is worth two in a keg.

Rodger had sold the Read to Be Thankful Bookshop for the second time, leaving me unemployed and soon to be broke. I had woken up to a "no need to go in – shop sold" text bleeping on my phone, accompanied by several of those annoying smiley faces.

I had no idea it was up for sale. When I say no idea, I mean I had ignored anything Rodger said that I didn't like. So when he said...

"I could work there until..."

"Please run until..."

"Will you take care until..."

I ignored anything said after the "until"... until, that is, the text with the smiley faces.

It had taken a while after the separation for us to be on civil terms again, and part of those civil terms was me taking care of the shop.

Originally, Rodger had arranged to sell the shop to a family friend of Shifty's who had plans to make it into a deli with chairs outside. The last thing Lochgilphead needed was a deli with chairs outside, especially when the deli was vegan.

Smoked tofu in Lochgilphead is as popular as sunscreen and outdoor swimming. There aren't many vegans in Lochgilphead, just as there are not many days when you can sit outside, especially next to a garage full of broken cars bound for the car cemetery. In the end, the sale fell through and Rodger asked me to run things until he could find another buyer, which I thought would take forever. Shops stand empty for years in Lochgilphead. In fact, it would probably be easier to sell a meat pie to a vegan than sell a shop in Lochgilphead.

Having stared at the text on and off all morning, I eventually decided to confront my ex. As I walked into the bar, he, in mid pint pull, looked up with a blank face.

"How can you spring this on me like this?" I said. "I love that shop."

"There is springing and there is ignoring," said Rodger, cryptically.

"And I could have taken over..." I muttered. "In time."

Which was not strictly true; I had as much chance of finding money for the shop as convincing Mavis that curry was haute cuisine.

"With your belly dancing?" said Rodger – not so cryptically. "There is only so much of that bullocks a town can take."

I watched him polish an already dry glass. He was not in good trim. He and Shifty had fallen out about the menu for the à la carte dining room. Turned out that Shifty was right and that steak tartare was a step too far for Lochgilphead.

Rodger was still sore from losing.

"And this time it's different," he snapped. "They want to keep it as a bookshop. And have already paid."

I looked at him.

"I – we need the money," he said, gesturing to the empty bar. "This place drinks it up."

"Typical," I said, looking at the only customer at the bar.

The old boy blinked and tilted his glass at me.

"And I can't afford to pay staff," he said. "Well – you, actually."

He began to talk about his plans with Shifty and how putting the Argyll on the map was high priority. "I need to focus on my artist talents – to save this place," he said. "It's our only hope."

I let out an over-the-top laugh, causing the old boy to choke on his pint.

"Priority," I said, "don't think so, just walked past 'entrepreneur of the year' in reception. He was flicking through Fyne fishing like he was at the dentist."

Which was not strictly true.

Shifty had been tossing out the out-of-date leaflets when I marched in. I stood with a "ready to do battle" stance, and he didn't even look up; instead, without a glance, he said, "Tell His Lordship I'll be in in a minute."

Can't remember the last time Shifty looked me in the eye. I think he'd rather I just went away. I used to think it was guilt, seeing as he had taken Rodger from me; now I realised it's more to do with his mother, Betty.

Betty spent her evenings in my garden with the Bag Lady, who lived there in a teepee. And according to Shifty, spending time in my garden was turning his mother into a stranger with weird ideas. And no matter how many times I told Shifty that I had as much influence on Betty and the Bag Lady as he did the weather, he still blamed me.

"My mother has turned into a lunatic raving about the afterlife and ghosts," he said. "And it's not healthy, her, an old woman sitting by the fire drinking *so-called* tea."

Rodger with his "I told you so" stance wasn't much help either.

I stared at my ex, snorting as he often does when grumpy. "It's a great offer and I would be a fool not to take it," he muttered, flicking off his tea towel.

I told him, "Withholding information was one of your most annoying talents," skipping the tempting; "not that you had many" insult.

Until he pointed out that he hadn't been withholding – I had not been listening. One of those moments where even one witness is one too many. The old boy watched me shrink as Rodger explained how many times he had told me.

"Splitting up is painful enough," I said, "without you rubbing it in."

Then Shifty entered, having heard the whole thing. He stood by his partner with his usual solidarity and told me that "the whole splitting issue was past tense" and that I should "move on." Then, he started to lecture me about how if I wasn't prepared to listen, what was the point of having a mobile?

"Why don't you get rid of your phone?" he said. "That would save you a bit."

I told him that I did listen "but sometimes with filters on," and Shifty with a loud tut snapped, "Filters – what next?"

I left after that, deciding to avoid the Argyll along with the new *soon-to-be-refurbished, soon-to-be-open, under-new-management* Read to Be Thankful. The truth was, without a wage I couldn't afford a packet of crisps, let alone a pint or a new book.

Here's me in the middle of menopause, living on last night's leftovers, while Rodger was talking about artistic licenses with a partner as loyal as a pit bull terrier.

I moaned to my pals and immediately regretted it. The Bag Lady told me I was exaggerating and should apply for benefits.

Mavis, having told me to listen to Rodger many times, said little apart from "I told you so," which I chose to ignore.

While Sheryl said I had fallen into victim mode and should find another job.

In the end, a job found me.

Chapter Four

THE FAVOUR

Dancing leads to many things, and not always an applause.

I was offered a job after a particularly impressive performance for an elderly couple. When I say impressive performance, it had little to do with dancing and more to do with cutting things short...a talent that has taken years to perfect.

A few days after I found out about Rodger's *sale of the century*, I was attempting to put a tenner of fuel into the car at Tesco's. I was grimly watching the dial when I heard "Nefertiti?" shouted across the tarmac with annoying urgency.

Mid tapping of the last drizzle, Jessie pulled at my arm.

A local fond of curry, wine, and gossip, Jessie had heard about my dancing. Her father was at the Argyll's old folk's do – years ago, where I had belly danced. Apparently he remembered little of it, apart from my name and how I looked as much like an Egyptian queen as a Scotch pie.

According to Jessie, he was on mood tablets at the time which, with just a whiff of whisky, could induce a coma, confusion, and/or both. He apparently woke with a bad taste in his mouth and everyone talking about Bingo (Shifty's dog) attacking Nefertiti's bra. A Turkish delight had hit him between the eyes, and before he had a chance to swear, another landed in his whisky. He left complaining bitterly about the inappropriate tossing of sweets, insisting that they appeared "from every crevice imaginable" and some he didn't know existed. Naturally the local paper made a meal of it, neglecting, of course, the mood tablets.

"It's a shame he missed you," she said. "He's a big fan of all things 'Eastern-ie.'"

"You could have fooled me," I said with a robust tap of the nozzle.

Jessie laughed. "Still talks about the Turkish delights."

"There were no crevices involved," I said, snapping the petrol cap shut.

"My father wouldn't know a crevice if it jumped up and bit his lip," said Jessie.

Which had me confused.

I went inside. Jessie, uninvited, tagged along. She followed me to the veg section.

"It's just that my father isn't in the greatest of health," said Jessie. "In fact, the chances of him seeing Christmas is as slim as those leeks over there."

I looked at a leek that any Welshman would've laughed at and immediately felt sorry for him.

"Mum's desperate," said Jessie. "She wants to give a send-off like no other."

"Send-off?" I said.

"I mean a party. He turns ninety-six and we've planned a curry."

"At the Taj?" I said, a little surprised.

"His love of naans goes back to his merchant navy years. And I've heard their naans are to die for."

"I thought it was the pakoras," I muttered, wondering if the leeks would last the night.

"He's just mad about Egypt," said Jessie. She touched my arm. "Then, when I saw you, it just sort of clicked..."

"Clicked?" I said.

"Can you do a dance for him – tomorrow?" said Jessie.

"At the Taj? That place is smaller than a portable loo."

"Not the Taj; Ban Duic in Inveraray. It is the sweetest place."

"I see," I muttered. "Well tomorrow is kind of short notice."

I picked up a leek and was just about to branch into the subject of a fee when Jessie's mother – or "the wife," as Jessie's father called her – approached with an "I dare you say no" strut.

"His time is limited," the wife said, "and he always wanted to go back somewhere desert-ie."

"Egypt, Mother, it's Egypt," said Jessie.

"And you're the nearest he'll ever get..." said the wife.

I continued to listen as they told me how much their dad "loved all things Middle Eastern but could hardly cough without passing out, let alone enjoy a shimmy."

I had no choice. I was cornered between the veg section and the cold meats. They were going nowhere until I said yes.

"Just do your best," muttered Jessie.

"But keep the Turkish delights out, and your stomach covered," said the wife. "He's got a dodgy heart..."

"Mum!" said Jessie.

"...can't remember the last time he saw a stomach," muttered the wife.

Jessie pushed an invitation card into my basket and began to steer her mother away.

"He falls asleep at the drop of anything," snapped Jessie. "A middle-aged stomach is hardly going to rouse him."

After they left, Mavis, who was loitering in the freezer section, came up and began to give me the low-down. She called "the wife" as tough as Chubby the butcher's steak...

"Married into wealth," said Mavis, "then hid it from everyone – the kids, the taxman, even slept with the VAT man to keep hold of it..."

"Aye right," I said.

"She is a woman you better not say no to," said Mavis. "And they pay well, tipped Lumpy big-time when he helped with a blocked drain."

I turned the invitation card over in my hand and wondered who made invitations for a curry.

"It's hardly an offer," I said, "and they never mentioned money."

"That's the rich for you," muttered Mavis, who went on about Lumpy's blocked drains and tipping all the way home. In fact, she went on about it so many times I was beginning to think she was on commission.

"Mavis," I said, "why do you care so much?"

"I could come along," she said. "It's been ages since we have done anything together."

I stared at the card. Why did she really want me to dance there? But before I had a chance to ask, she was out of the car and flicking my kettle on.

Chapter Five

MAVIS'S HOPE

A good woman knows when she's beat; and a smart woman exits before anyone else finds out.

The birthday party was held in Ban Duic, an Indian restaurant, thirty miles away in a sweet little town called Inveraray. A restaurant posh enough for not only one massive chandelier but chandeliers in each corner and large mirrors on each wall – the sort that required a joiner to install. It was an airy (some would call freezing) place with large old-fashioned windows looking out onto Loch Fyne on one wall and the public toilets on the other. It had beautiful wooden tables, matching uncomfortable seats, and a heaving wine list with prices that probably paid for the expensive interior and the owner's brand-new BMW.

Thirty miles and thirty minutes of Mavis...in a mood that was hard to pin down.

She was sucking on a Rennie while flicking through a catalogue of dresses from Pakistan and with each flick came another crunch, another sigh, another tut...

"They are cheap, I give you that," she muttered.

I didn't answer. When Mavis tuts, it's always best to leave her to it.

"And colourful, no waistline, that's a bonus. I mean look at that." She flashed a page in my face. "What do you think, Neff?"

"Mavis, I'm driving," I said.

She let out another tut as I continued to stare in front of me.

"I decided to wear a scarf," she finally said.

"I thought you've had enough of scarves."

"Lumpy's idea." She sighed. "But I'm not wrapping it around my head like he wants."

"I see."

She slapped the brochure shut. "Lumpy wants to Indian up the community centre with a few cushions and pictures from the after-school club. Pictures of some village in Pakistan the children support."

Mavis forced a smile.

"I never realised Lumpy could be so obsessional. I mean, Pakistan in crayon – what next, a yogi to marry us?"

I said nothing.

"I agreed to a few pakoras, but not all this...this...joss stick sort of stuff."

She slipped a Rennie into her mouth and began to flick again.

I did think about answering – suggesting that she speak to Lumpy about the whole joss stick issue – when Mavis continued...

"I mean I am just not happy," she said. "There is a place for spice and a wedding isn't it. And before you say anything, I told Lumpy. He didn't listen, instead he rumbled on about how the chef must cook the banquet. Apparently his fish is to die for."

Mavis began to flick with vengeance.

"Two months ago you thought a curry was a great idea. What's changed?" I said.

"He's taken over, the chef, it's not my wedding anymore, it's Tenzam's...and Lumpy's."

"Tenzam?" I said. "Find that hard to believe, doesn't look the marrying kind." I waited for her to laugh.

She sighed. "That Tenzam has ruined my life," said Mavis with drama. "He's always speaking in Bengali, which I'm sure is about me, and Lumpy understands. I mean how? He says it's all in the body language."

Mavis tutted.

"Body language? Why don't you read mine, I said, then he called me childish – me, childish, that's ridiculous. I'm the sensible one. I'm not the one wanting to sit on the floor."

"What's wrong with sitting on the floor?" I said. "We used to do it all the time in class."

"This is different, I'll be dressed up."

"But you're getting a dress from Pakistan, it'll be made for sitting on the floor."

Mavis tossed the catalogue into the back of the car. "I would like to take that Tenzam's spicy dip and shove it," she snapped.

I gave up and put an Immortal Egypt CD on a relaxing low.

She smiled. "I'm going to have a chat with the owner."

"What?"

"Of Ban Duic," said Mavis.

"Why?" I said, steering the car into the car park.

Mavis pointed to an obvious car space like I couldn't see it. "Yes," she said. "He needs to know what's going on."

I stared at the public toilets ahead. Radio One was blasting from the janitor's office. A few local boys were kicking a ball aimlessly about, which every now and then trailed into the public toilets...

"That'll do," shouted the janitor.

None took any notice.

"What do you have planned," I muttered.

"Just a word about how Tenzam is getting too friendly, suggest swapping chefs." She sighed. "I just want my Lumpy back."

The janitor stood at the door with a menacing look and shouted, "That'll do, any more and I'll have you."

I stepped out of the car clutching a dance cane, iPad, and bag overflowing with my jingly costume.

The janitor shouted, "Mind the ball."

I turned, tripped, and swore.

Mavis smiled. "Don't worry, I won't ruin your performance."

It hadn't even occurred to me that she would, until she said it...

❋

The wife you couldn't say no to tapped on the window. "Quick, before anyone sees you," she hissed and gestured to the back door.

I made for the back of the restaurant and the daughter ushered me into the store – a place as suitable for changing as a butcher's shop.

It smelt of garlic and spice and required a contortionist to manoeuvre in, as well as Mavis at the door not only holding it shut but barking at any who tried to enter.

Until she saw the manager...

I had barely taken my jacket off let alone adjusted my hair when the wife who can't be ignored barged in with an "are you ready" stance.

"The pudding's finished," she said. "And he's starting to nod off. You'll need to hurry, or his carer will be back to pick him up."

Two bumps and a stubbed toe later, I stepped out of the store, hopped a puddle, sidestepped the bin, and passed the chef outside having a fag.

Mavis had disappeared.

He coughed, tossed his sucked-to-death cigarette to one side, slid another between his lips, and turned to face me.

He was the ugliest man I had ever met.

He wore waist-high jeans and had dark slicked-back fifties hair. Years of smoking had leathered up his face and given him a cough like a tuberculous warning. He stank of smoke and had a downturned Mick Jagger mouth, probably from grimacing since he was born. He slipped on a white wrinkled chef's jacket and looked at me.

"She wants me to work in that dump of a place," he said in a Glaswegian accent. He flicked his cigarette butt an inch from my foot. "As if."

I was about to attempt a joke about free takeaway, but I realised he wasn't even listening. He was staring at the local boys still kicking the ball about.

Chapter Six

THE DANCE

A dancer is only as good as her audience.

Mavis was standing at the bar in the restaurant talking to Kamal, the owner. He was slim, dark, and handsome in an Imran Khan sort of way. He poured her a coffee and slid a few dinner mints across the bar like they were something elicit. Mavis slid a mint between her lips like it was something to be savoured and smiled back.

Their eyes met.

I stood by the fryer wondering what the hell Mavis was playing at. We only had an hour on the parking meter, and there she was miles from my music player acting like she was on a speed-dating night.

"Music," I shouted, which she greeted with an "in a minute" gesture.

Jessie, the daughter, shouted at the birthday dad to "wake up."

The birthday dad was sitting at the centre of the restaurant with all eyes on him. Not that he noticed; he was too busy trying to negotiate his extra-large seventies tie that someone had lassoed around his neck. It was pink and shiny and seemed to itch about his neck, as Birthday Dad could not stop pulling at it.

"Leave it alone," snapped his wife with a slap of his fingers.

Birthday Dad didn't hear; his bony fingers fluttered uselessly about the cemented knot of the tie. A relative walked by and patted his shoulder. He looked up and saw Mavis talking to Kamal and flashed half a dozen yellow teeth.

"It's you," he shouted. "Can you help me with this tie?"

Mavis, used to such elderly folk in the post office, gave him a paternal wave and continued talking to Kamal.

"The Taj Mahal could do with a man like him," she said.

Kamal looked at Birthday Dad, confused.

Mavis pointed to the chef. "He would be way better than that Tenzam."

Chef, who had creeped up next to me, snorted. "As if."

"It's her all right," shouted Birthday Dad, "the one who saved me." He tugged at the tie. "Give us a hand, I'm getting strangulated!"

The wife slapped his hand again.

Mavis's smile dropped.

"Dad, it's not her," said Jessie, "she's too old."

Jessie looked about the room, shamefaced. "He's talking about that healer, with herbs. He's not himself anymore, it's the tablets."

"She saved my life, so she did, I'd be dead if it wasn't for that Fanny," said Birthday Dad, gesturing to Mavis. "That's what she told me, 'You'd be dead if it wasn't for me.'"

A few of the guests nodded vaguely...

Birthday Dad got up and was about to head for Mavis when he was stopped by his daughter.

"That's not Fanny, it's her sister," she said.

Mavis has a sister? I had no idea.

"Give us a hand, Fanny," he shouted.

Mavis's face darkened. She flicked the music on and turned it up high and gestured for me to start.

The wife pushed her husband back down on his seat.

"This is for you," she snapped. "Nefertiti, all the way from Egypt."

Birthday Dad looked up with fright.

The drums began to pound as I entered. There wasn't much room to dance, so I placed a bowl on my head and went for a few balancing moves...

"Watch out for the Turkish delights," shouted Birthday Dad and pulled a napkin over his head.

The dance didn't go as planned. In fact, nothing did …

For a start, Birthday Dad had forgotten all about Egypt and naan breads and instead – thanks to Mavis looking like her sister – could not forget Fanny.

Fanny ran a clinic in Glasgow and according to Jessie was a "trailblazer of herbs and the like." She had treated the whole of Jessie's family, including her dad, whose long-term back condition was finally cured with fingertip acupuncture.

After years of creeping about like the Hunchback of Notre Dame, Birthday Dad was finally back to marching like a sergeant and spent most of his time doing just that – driving "the wife" crazy.

Birthday Dad went from doing little but pressing the TV remote to parading about the garden with the dog, shouting "left right left." Or marching into the kitchen demanding dinner, despite having just eaten lunch. And the wife was fed up.

She pulled the napkin from Birthday Dad. He peered past my shoulder at Mavis.

"Fanny," he shouted.

Mavis, however, was sulking. Apparently looking like her sister was a cross she had to bear and she hated being reminded of it. In the end, with a packet of after-dinner mints, Kamal and Mavis finally convinced Birthday Dad that there were no flying Turkish delights.

Mavis loosened his tie and told him that Nefertiti was her "pal," then turned the music on.

I did my best and moved about the tables with a pretty good saunter while the chef retreated to the back door and lit his millionth cigarette.

At the same time, the local lads who had been told "that'll do" once too often by the janitor dribbled their ball around the back of the restaurant. Their scuffling and laughing could be heard over the drumming until Mavis turned the music up.

"Bit loud," snapped the wife as Birthday Dad began to shout, "left right left."

"Kick it here," shouted the chef to one of the local boys, and before he had time to spit out his fag, the ball landed smack into his face – sending his fag flying. And he, without a blink, head-butted it back.

The ball bounced off the "dressing shed," into the kitchen, off a fryer, and, accompanied by a fair amount of sizzling, into the restaurant.

The chef followed.

Birthday Dad was now on his feet, marching on the spot, shouting "left right left." Jessie told him to be quiet, while the wife slapped his fingers.

"Up yours," Birthday Dad said. "That's marching music, isn't it, Fanny?"

"Dad, it's Egyptian, for the lady to dance to..."

"Up yours," he shouted again just as the ball rolled past his foot.

Birthday dad's face lit up...he went for a kick.

The crowd hushed...as the Egyptian drum, still on full pelt, reached a climax of frenzied beating.

Jessie saw the ball.

She went for a low "kick it out of the way of dad" manoeuvre as the wife went for a "stop Birthday Dad" lunge and slap – both of which missed Birthday Dad.

He, ducking the wife's slap, missed the ball.

His feet skidded into a tap dance, kicking Jessie. She grabbed her mother's now-redundant Zimmer and tried to move out of the way. It overbalanced, and Jessie crashed on top of it, knocking into Birthday Dad.

Birthday Dad stumbled, tripped, almost gained his balance, then made for the "no-longer-there" Zimmer, grabbing the tablecloth instead...

Cutlery, plates, and curry crashed to the floor, followed by a selection of dips and Birthday Dad.

"Watch out!"

"Look out!"

"*Mind!!*"

Birthday Dad looked up to the heavens. "Fanny," he muttered as chicken tikka masala followed in slow plops onto his chest...

The music stopped...

"That'll not wash out," muttered a voice from the back as Jessie, with a sickly, squishy sound, skidded to her feet and then slipped again.

Chapter Seven

A NEW PLAN

Beware of 'helpful' friends they often forget who they are trying to help.

As Birthday Dad lay prostrate on the floor, I turned off the music. I gave the wife a few of my stress buster's herbal teabags I always carry with me *and never used* and patted her on the arm. I almost felt for the wife; the only woman her husband wanted was Fanny. Even as he lay on the floor, eyes glazed with a twisted limb, he wanted her.

"Fanny, can you hear me..."

"Fanny, are you there..."

"I'm done for, Fanny..."

"Fanny...*Fanny!*"

The chef swept into the room, brandishing a broom. He ripped the head off, cracked the handle in half across his knee, and shouted, "Call an ambulance."

A few winced but the chef didn't flinch. He pulled a cloth from a table; plates and cutlery crashed to the floor; the chef said nothing. With a swift brush of his arm he swept the crockery to one side and knelt by Birthday Dad.

Jessie – a woman who had sworn off men for a decade – was spellbound. She watched as the chef gently wrapped the tablecloth around Birthday Dad's leg using the broom handle as a splint.

"Heavens," she muttered with a long sigh.

The chef casually flicked a few grains of rice from Birthday Dad's chin.

"Is that comfortable?" he whispered.

"What?" shouted Birthday Dad.

"Have you any pain?" the chef said louder.

"What? Where is Fanny?"

The chef pointed to his disfigured leg. "Does it hurt?"

"Left, right...oh, bugger!" Shouted Birthday Dad

The chef's bulldog face softened and Jessie cooed.

"Don't move," shouted the chef.

Birthday Dad began to pant.

The chef turned to Jessie with a look of concern which had even me impressed. "Something wet," he said.

Jessie raced for her bag, rummaged, pulled, and reached across to the chef with a trembling hand. "Here," she whispered.

Their hands touched across a baby wipe. Their eyes met, Jessie's chest heaved, and for a moment the chef paused with a smile of splendid teeth.

"Perfect," he said.

"Thank you," she said with a flushed look.

Birthday Dad coughed, spluttered, and shouted, "Fanny – they haven't a clue," and he continued to shout as the ambulance boys finally wheeled him away.

I watched along with Mavis as the family silently trailed behind Birthday Dad on his stretcher. Jessie, clutching the chef's arm, threw me a weak smile. "Hardly a dance," she muttered.

"Exactly," snapped the wife, clutching her Zimmer. She threw a glare at Mavis. "And that was no music."

I sulked back to the shed to change, trying not to think about the waste of an afternoon. I didn't even get a tip, let alone my un-agreed fee. I was in the middle of folding my costume into my bag perched on a slab of tinned mangoes when Mavis bounded in muttering about "the chef" and "a second plan of attack."

"Well he's not for moving," she said, not looking the least bit upset. "Looks like he and that Jessie have hit it off and she lives here."

"He had no intention of moving anyway," I muttered.

"He likes you," Mavis said.

"The chef? Funny way of showing it, spitting cigarettes at my feet."

"He said you handle yourself well."

"Well what do you expect when someone tosses a cigarette at you, a round of applause?"

Mavis watched me slide on my jacket with a quiet hum and then began to button me up...

"He even called you an asset," she said with a final dusting about my shoulders.

"Well at my stage in life that's a given," I snapped.

"Come back in for a drink," said Mavis.

"Don't think so."

"He wants to see you... and he's poured you one."

"The chef?"

"No. Kamal."

The owner passed me a superb cappuccino along with a smile that was impossible to resist.

The ambulance was still outside with the engine running. The wife was outside with Jessie and the chef; she was banging on the door telling the "birthday boy" to "do what he was told and mind to not lose the tie."

"Not many would think about a herbal in such a situation," Kamal said.

"I like to think on my feet," I muttered.

He looked at the chef, who was now consoling Jessie. The back door of the ambulance opened – the pink tie appeared, followed by a final echo – "Fanny, I'm coming!" – from Birthday Dad.

The wife clutched the tie as the door closed.

We watched the ambulance drive off.

"I could use a woman like you," said Kamal.

"Sorry?"

"Yes, you'd be an asset in a restaurant," he said, sliding a plate of mints my way.

Mavis threw me a "told you so" look.

I looked around the posh restaurant and saw myself laughing with tourists, serving posh bubbly and Gaelic coffees – right up my street.

"Thank you," I said.

"A woman like you would never get flustered, and Mavis says that you are a woman who gets things done, who doesn't take any – how did you put it, Mavis…backchat?"

"Well I wouldn't say that," I muttered, thinking about earning money again. "But I am sure I have a sari-type dress somewhere.

"That won't be necessary." He smiled. "The Taj Mahal is mainly takeaway, very small. No one will care what you are wearing."

I stared ahead as the chef, Jessie, and the wife headed off behind the ambulance.

"Taj Mahal," I muttered, "in Lochgilphead?"

"Great place, very local," said Kamal.

He leant closer to me; garlic and Old Spice wafted past. "Tenzam needs keeping an eye on and Mavis says you're just the woman for that."

"What?"

Mavis, standing behind Kamal, gave me the thumps-up. She had exactly the same smile as he did…

Chapter Eight

THE TAKEAWAY

When it comes to pakoras, size always matters.

A week later I was filling tubs with spicy onions and mint dips like a pro.

Turns out all Kamal's talk of me "handling things" was just that – talk. Wendy who used to work in the takeaway took a job in the co-op and everyone else he asked laughed at him.

Still, Mavis was pleased. "Two birds," she said. "You and me, you a new job – and I can come and see you all the time – keep an eye on things."

I had my doubts; in my experience, keeping an eye on things was never that simple, and I had enough trouble getting used to my new job.

I spent the first week answering the phone while trying to get to grips with a menu as easy to understand as a TV remote. I served food, cleared up food, and did a million other food chores, in a way as foreign to me as the menu. I was thinking on my feet in a whole new non-dancer way and, to be honest, not enjoying it.

For a start, the Taj Mahal was small, with a kitchen the size of a dog kennel and a restaurant the size of a Wendy tent. The "Wendy tent," which had three tables squashed into a two-table space, was as easy to serve in as tap dancing on ice. Taking out plates of food required sidestepping with plates held high above my head on a floor that, with just a whiff of moisture, turned into an ice rink. And the plates were kept in an old fridge which required a good kick to shut – not easy when you're balancing a selection of dips – mid skid while explaining to one of the many locals that...

"Yes, I still do belly dancing, but no classes at the moment."

"No, it wasn't me that did the ole boy in, it was a football."

"No, I haven't got rid of the Bag Lady yet."

"Yes, I have left the bookshop, and I have no idea who is taking it over."

It was a job I never saw myself doing, done in front of a public I knew too well.

My first shift was spent answering the phone to...

"It's yourself, at the Taj?"

"You still at the Taj?"

"Is this the bookshop? I thought it was the Taj."

And the second shift was spent answering the phone to...

"You still there?"

"You haven't poisoned anyone yet?"

"Is this the bookshop? I thought it was the Indian."

My first week was spent mastering the art of "adding up" (their till was away "getting fixed") while learning the difference between a balti, a bhuna, and all the others in between.

The second week was adjusting to a till that crashed open at the speed of light while still trying to understand the difference between a balti, a bhuna, and all the others in between.

And the third was pretending I knew.

Tenzam asked me to write down the names of each customer, which at first was as difficult to remember as the curries.

"James from Kilmichael – Pete from Whitehouse – Barbara from next door." Tenzam knew them all, and their taste buds.

Tenzam was a master at pleasing, and his curries were addictive. Every night he made me something delicious, and by the third week not only was I addicted but so was the Bag Lady, who started issuing orders...

"Mild tonight, and no lamb, it repeats on me."

"Just a small portion of rice tonight, and can you throw in a couple of those pakoras?"

While Betty, keeping an eye on her waistline, insisted on no ghee, no cream, and definately no poppadums.

The Roadworks Man came every night. He always sat in the same most in-the-way spot possible, with his "despite the weather" wet work jacket dumped in the perfect tripping position for me. And as I tripped over his shoes, skidded across his straps, or kicked his backpack or whatever else was sprawled across the floor, he'd tut *like it was my fault* with a "mind yourself" while staring at the menu like he had never seen it before.

And he always ordered the same things.

Come to think of it, most people did – except for Lumpy.

Lumpy, who usually appeared mid "hmm, delicious" from the Roadworks Man, had worked his way through the entire menu. Even the coffees.

But that didn't stop him reading the menu like it was Shakespeare.

Lumpy had even tried some of the staff curries, which pleased Tenzam no end. He loved talking about Bangladeshi food, and he was happy to indulge Lumpy with deep-fried lentil parcels, dhal like his mother made, and biriyani fit for royalty.

Tonight was no different...

Lumpy skipped through the entrance, avoiding any "catching of the heels" from the door "with a life of its own." A knack he, like most locals, did without thinking.

Tenzam appeared, rubbing his hands on his apron. "Special Bangladesh fish, just for you," he said.

Lumpy shook the rain from his jacket, pulled up a chair by the Roadworks Man, and glanced at his empty plate. "You had the usual then," said Lumpy.

"Hmm, delicious," said the Roadworks Man.

Tenzam asked Lumpy where Mavis was.

I already knew the answer; Mavis, under protest, was living on anything but curries and was either at the chippie or at home boiling up an egg.

"She doesn't want to discuss food?" said Tenzam with a shocked look. Discussing food was his favourite topic.

"She's busy," said Lumpy with a blank expression.

"Do you not think a bride being too busy to discuss her own banquet is maybe a sign?" I said.

"Of what?" said Lumpy.

"That she isn't happy."

"Happy?"

"With the whole curry thing."

"What? Oh that. That's just talk," said Lumpy. "Mavis is all for a curry, she's even talking about us sitting on the floor."

I wondered what planet Lumpy was on.

Lumpy accepted his Nescafé from Tenzam, who pulled up a chair next to Lumpy.

"What you need is fish – like my mother's – good vegetables and maybe a special biriyani," said Tenzam, sipping his tea.

"What about Mavis?" I said. "Did she not say the last thing she wanted was fish?"

"Yes, well, there is fish and then there is Tenzam's fish, huh, Tenzam?"

"You want extra chillies, fresh green are best."

Lumpy laughed, and he was in the middle of making a joke about spicing up the wedding night when Mavis walked in.

She looked frazzled. The sort of frazzled that was best ignored. So I started to fold napkins as she stood by the counter, huffing.

She tossed another peppermint into her mouth.

"You hungry?" Tenzam said to Mavis.

Mavis looked at him like he was the reason for all her woes. "No," she said. "I have eaten."

"I am," I said.

Tenzam looked at me. "What would you like?" he shouted. Tenzam always shouted.

"Anything with mushrooms," I said, "or chickpeas – I'm off meat."

Within minutes, he placed a plate of fish unknown in front of me, and another in front of Lumpy. The dark sauce didn't hide the head.

I caught Mavis's eye.

"Don't know why he asks." I attempted a small laugh. "I tell him what I want and then he gives me something completely different – in an instant, like it was already made."

"Men," muttered Mavis with a glare at Lumpy.

"Why ask if you don't listen?" I said. I looked at Mavis. "I've given up trying to be a vegan."

Mavis stared at the fish head, repulsed.

"This is real Bangladesh curry," said Lumpy, "isn't it, Tenzam?"

"Once it was living and breathing, now it's slaughtered and sliced," said Mavis.

"It's fish from Bangladesh – the best in the world," said Lumpy.

"Slaughtered fish," said Mavis.

"Everything is slaughtered in the end," huffed Tenzam, who returned to the kitchen and turned his radio up.

I told Mavis yet again that I had given up the whole vegan thing and she didn't even let me finish...

"There'll be no fish eyes at my wedding," she shouted at the kitchen; Tenzam turned the radio up even louder.

"There is more to a fish than its eye," said Lumpy, nodding at the Roadworks Man, "isn't that right?"

The Roadworks Man was about to say something but stopped.

Mavis's frazzled look had turned to more of a glare...

Chapter Nine

THE SISTER

Love is blind until you have to share the TV remote.

Since the Birthday Dad incident, Fanny had been on the phone to Mavis several times. Birthday Dad spent his time in hospital shouting for Fanny, and Fanny wanted to "get things right" before "stepping into the opposition," as she called it.

"We haven't talked in years," said Mavis to Lumpy, "and now it's more times than your trip to the takeaway. I told her all I know but will she listen? Look, I said, I am in the middle of a wedding crisis, I don't have time for all this. Could have kicked myself, now she wants to know all about my wedding."

"Oh, she knew before that," said Lumpy.

"What?" said Mavis.

"Yes, she is helping me source things," said Lumpy.

"Things? What things?"

"It's a surprise," said Lumpy with a mouthful of rice.

Tenzam came out again, his face lighting up. "Roast chicken?" he said. "Everyone loves roast chicken."

"Roast chicken?" said Mavis with a hint of hope.

"Bangladesh style," said Tenzam, "very tasty."

"Oh," said Mavis. "So is it spicy then?"

"Yes, but very little," said Tenzam.

"You like spice," said Lumpy.

"Yes, but spicy roast chicken? That's a step too far. Roast chicken has potatoes, stuffing, and lemon. It's not spicy, it's...herby."

"You can never go too far with curry," said the Roadworks Man.

Lumpy laughed.

I tried to placate Mavis by offering her a few poppadums. "The mint sauce is mild," I said. Mavis didn't even hear.

"I don't want a takeaway wedding," she said.

"This is no takeaway," snapped Tenzam, "this is special wedding feast – Bangladesh style."

Mavis looked unconvinced.

Tenzam returned to the kitchen.

Shifty told Mavis she had insulted a good man doing a good turn with fabulous food. "We're just trying to make a great day," he said.

"For whom?" she asked.

Lumpy said nothing.

Mavis then told him he didn't understand and left, threatening eggs on toast.

I was beginning to feel a headache coming on; keeping an eye on things always did that to me. And Mavis had a look on her face I had not seen since the famous rugby club incident, an incident Lumpy knew nothing about...

Chapter Ten

ONE WHISKY IS ONE TOO MANY

It takes a special type of person to drink whisky, angry folk are not them.

That night I went home and handed the Bag Lady her takeaway. She had a cold and was not in good trim.

I told the Bag Lady that chilli was good for a cold. She opened the bag with an unimpressed look and followed me into the kitchen.

"Your Mavis turned up," she said. The Bag Lady always said "your" when my friends cheesed her off.

I sat at the table and looked at my unopened Jaipuri.

"She wouldn't leave," said the Bag Lady, "wanted more whisky."

"And you gave it to her?" I said.

"I gave her a hot chocolate."

I sighed. The Bag Lady's hot chocolates were as alcoholic as a cocktail and had knocked the legs off me more than once.

"She was upset," said the Bag Lady. "And you were no help..."

"Help? I did my best – it's not easy helping Mavis," I said.

The Bag Lady sniffed. "You were supposed to keep an eye on things."

"I offered her a mint dip..." I muttered.

The Bag Lady pulled up a seat and began to open the Jaipuri.

The Bag Lady and Betty had been tucking into hot chocolate when

Mavis arrived. With a quick glance at Mavis's downcast face, Betty had offered her one and poured "extra" whisky in it.

Then Lumpy had phoned and began to tell Mavis not to worry about Tenzam as he wasn't in least offended about her and her roast chicken. In fact, he said he was toying with the idea of duck, which according to the Bag Lady sent Mavis into a spin.

"What's duck got to do with it," she shouted across the garden, and then went into a tirade about "real stuffing."

I asked the Bag Lady how many hot chocolates Mavis had had and she looked sheepish.

"She sort of went onto the whisky after one, maybe two," said the Bag Lady, poking at the red sauce.

"I see," I said.

"And then Betty left."

I let out a sigh. Mavis is one of those people who should never even sniff a whisky, let alone drink it, especially when emotional. Whisky turns Mavis into a "she-devil" and required specialised sarcasm and timed ignoring to control, something only a best friend can do. And something that a partner, no matter how hard he practises, will never achieve. In fact, a partner when his woman is in she-devil mode is best to run for the hills and let the best friend deal with the whole thing.

"You did your best," I muttered.

Mavis in she-devil mode has been seen by few and talked about by many. In fact, I had only heard about it from others until the famous rugby club incident, after which Mavis vowed never to touch the stuff again.

It was a few years ago, when Lumpy was a mere flirtation in Mavis's life. The rugby club had been invited to perform a dance for a charity benefit, and Mavis, Sheryl, and I had been asked to teach them a routine. "A free football for every poor kid in Scotland" was the aim of the benefit, and somehow half a dozen men doing the "Dance of the Seven Veils" was deemed the best way to raise the money.

Mavis was all for it. She threw herself into the rehearsals, creating a funny scarf routine performed to the sixties James Bond theme. It took several nights for the team to master, and Mavis glowed; comedy along with scarves, it seemed, was her thing.

The captain was so impressed and grateful he invited us to not only watch the performance but join "the lads" for a drink afterwards. Mavis and Sheryl tucked into the whisky, sampling all three malts, and Mavis was laughing with the rest of us until the captain mentioned Fanny.

"You remind me of her," he said. "You move the same."

"Fanny," snapped Mavis. "That woman moves like a plank. How could you say I move like her?"

The captain shifted uncomfortably. "It was meant as a compliment. She's a young thing, who massaged the team after the game."

"I know who she is."

"And you move like..." His voice faded as he saw "laugh a minute" Mavis now glowering like a dog over a bone. He looked confused.

"I think you will find it is she who moves like me," snapped Mavis. "If she is lucky."

Mavis downed her whisky and pushed the empty glass toward the bar for another, then nodded at Sheryl for a refill.

Sheryl shook her head.

"I mean she must be half your age," ventured another brave player, "and yet..." He looked at her dark face. "...you're quite..." His voice trailed off. "...similar..."

"As similar as your free balls for children are to a real football," snapped Mavis, now standing with a "ready to do battle" stance.

"What the hell is wrong with you?" said Sheryl.

"Probably needing a good shag," muttered a voice from the back.

Mavis turned on the crowd of men. "A shag? Is that what you think I need?"

The men hushed. The whole bar stared at her. She looked about from one to another. "That's what you think − I need a good frigging seeing to?" She huffed. "As if!"

"Come on, Mavis, we were having a good time," said Sheryl.

"Yes, a good time being told I look like some stuck-up cow who moves like a stunned penguin."

"I like Fanny," said the voice from the back. "She sorted my back."

"Who's Fanny?" I whispered to Sheryl.

"While," continued Mavis, "being offered a seeing to by men who think prancing about in a scarf is the high art of comedy."

"No one's offering you a shag," said another voice from the back.

Sheryl told Mavis to drink up but she sipped annoyingly slow – scanning for the voice at the back.

"Look, lady," said the barman, "we don't want any trouble. This is a respectable place."

Which even I thought a tad exaggerated; it had the air of shady deals and after-hours drinking, along with a "Ladies" full of plastic flowers that hadn't seen a duster in decades.

"Hardly respectable," snapped Mavis. "Chicken in a basket and three choices of whiskies."

"Right, that's it – out."

"I mean look at this menu – laughable."

"Come on, out you get, and you can take these two so-called dancers with you," said the barman.

"So-called dancers...we are the crème de la crème," said Mavis with an angry flick of her scarf.

"At your age, the only cream you'll get is on top of a fruit pie," said the barman.

A few of "the lads" sniggered.

"Now out," shouted the barman, who was now standing at an opened exit door.

I silently led my pal into the car and drove her home without a word. And it wasn't until a few days later that I asked her, "What was all that carry-on about?"

"Don't remember anything," she said with a blank face, "must have been the whisky. All I remember was how horrible their chicken in the basket was."

Sheryl and I did sometimes wonder, and we made a pact to give the whisky a "wide berth" when Mavis was about. It was only when I was started in the takeaway that I met the rugby captain again. He graciously greeted Mavis like nothing happened and she graciously pretended to have forgotten, and none of us mentioned Fanny.

Lumpy, however, also knew Fanny. He had met her a few times while visiting Mavis's mother with Mavis. He thought Fanny would be perfect to help create the wedding of the century, and Mavis was as happy about that as she was with Tenzam's cooked fish eyes.

"She went mental over the phone," said the Bag Lady, "shouting, 'Why don't you marry him...her...it then?' I never seen her like that before..."

"I have," I muttered.

"She planted herself by the fire, all red and tearful, and no way was she moving." The Bag Lady sighed, looking out onto the garden. "I had to do something, so I told her she could stay the night, as walking to the couch was probably all she could manage."

"Yes, I am sure that would have made her feel better."

Puss jumped as Mavis, clutching her whisky, entered the room with a slam and a glum look on par with Tenzam's when he gets his pay packet.

I said nothing, and this time neither did the Bag Lady.

Chapter Eleven

STRICTLY FRIENDS

There is listening, and there is looking like your listening; both require a drink.

"Thanks for letting me stay," Mavis said with tearful eyes. "Lumpy and I had a terrible row. He seems to think he knows what I want without asking."

"He wants to surprise you," I said.

"Yes," said the Bag Lady, pushing a glass of water Mavis's way, "Lumpy just cares."

"So he asks Fanny?" said Mavis.

"She's your sister," said the Bag Lady, pushing the water closer.

Mavis looked from the Bag Lady to me. "Fanny has as much idea about what I want as Tenzam."

I slid the whisky from Mavis's hand. She pulled it back and took a sip.

"I told him he was not thinking about me at all. 'You should have asked,' I said. And do you know what he said?"

The Bag Lady and I shook our heads.

"I thought you love curry." She leant back in her chair waiting for a response.

"Loving a bhuna in front of *Strictly*," I said, "is one thing, but that doesn't mean I want to say 'I do' over it."

The Bag Lady looked at me questioningly.

"*Strictly Come Dancing*, a TV show; some say it's better than going out."

Mavis emptied her whisky. "Then he started waffling on about Tenzam's special wedding feast," she sipped, "and I sort of lost it." She looked at me. "I mean three types of rice and everything in Bengali batter—it's hardly fine dining, is it?"

I pushed the Jaipuri towards the Bag Lady. She pushed it back.

"Tea," I said, and the Bag Lady moved to flick on the kettle.

A year ago, Lumpy and Mavis had settled into domestic bliss without a backward glance – and I watched, recovering from the loss of my Rodger. They did everything together; they were a happy couple. Lumpy even visited Mavis's mother with her, who was in a care home and slowly losing her memory.

While Mavis had a man who could "turn his hand to anything," I had the Bag Lady sleeping in my garden talking about independence like it was the be-all and end-all.

"No one should share their toolbox," she'd say, usually when I was moaning about being alone and having to fix things myself.

Her advice was rubbish...I mean what artist like me wants to spend their time unblocking drains and mowing the lawn? I want someone else to do that while I do something more interesting. I don't want to spend half the day trying to work out which fuse goes where. I wanted to spend half the day doing yoga and then cooking something for a man who thought I was worth having sex with. Now I sleep alone. Even Puss had moved on.

I was so jealous of Mavis that it hurt; there were days when I couldn't even smile at her. And she was so loved up she didn't even notice. She even gave me her toolbox – dumped it on my kitchen table one day with a great big fat smile.

"Don't need this anymore," she said, "Lumpy fixed things while I made the coffee."

I stared at Mavis as she downed the last of her whisky. It had taken a long time to stop feeling sorry for myself, learning to make do. And now poor old Mavis, if she wasn't careful, would go through the same thing.

Not something you would wish on anyone, let alone your best pal.

Chapter Twelve

THE TAJ MAHAL

A great pakora doesn't always require a dip.

A couple of weeks later, I walked into the co-op. Tenzam had grown accustomed to me and saw me as someone who could do more than just answer the phone. I could also pick things up from the co-op, put electricity onto his card, and even go to the post office for him with large parcels to Bangladesh which seemed to cost next to nothing to send. And, no matter how much I explained that this was not my job, he would smile his sweet smile and I would give in.

Most people gave in with Tenzam.

Tenzam looked younger than his forty-plus years and spoke English in a literal fashion which made him sound sincere and innocent. He had a round smiley face with smooth brown skin and the ability to look not only like he was listening but like he understood. In fact, he was the reason most people came in. Some even refused to leave until Tenzam came out to speak to them...

"Tarzan about?"

"You there, Tarzan?"

No one pronounced his name properly and Tenzam never seemed to notice. Instead, he would answer every 'Tarzan' with a full smile, as if it was his real name. And no matter how busy he was, if someone wanted to see him, he would poke his head around the kitchen door and nod. Sometimes he would even come out, wipe his hands on his apron, shake, and listen like they were the most important person in the world.

Except when Kamal was there.

Kamal shouted at everyone and everything. He shouted at his car, his phone, even the restaurant's massive gas cooker. And on a really bad day, Kamal would shout at all three along with anyone that got in his way. In Kamal's world, chefs were meant to be seen and not heard, and demands to see "Tarzan" were greeted with a "he is cooking" grunt.

I stood at the checkout with several tins of shaving foam, half a dozen toothbrushes, five packets of toothpaste, and a mountain of Dove cream soap. Tenzam was making a box to send home, and toiletries, it seemed, were the pièce de résistance. Wendy threw me one of her "been there done that" looks as I began to empty my basket.

"You still there then," she said.

I placed the last of the toothbrushes on the counter. "Yes."

"Don't know how you can stand it, my clothes always smelt like spice city," she laughed.

"I quite like the smell," I lied.

"I mean I am not a racist," she said.

"Nobody is these days," I said.

"But they don't make it easy."

I watched her as she robotically flicked through one toothbrush several times, shoved the rest into a bag, and expertly twirled the bag around and tied a knot, just how Tenzam liked it. "No free curry is worth that carry-on," she said, dumping the bag on the counter.

"Carry-on?"

"Aye, creeping about a kitchen the size of a wardrobe – albeit a walk-in wardrobe." She snorted at her wit.

"Oh that."

"Trying not to get shouted at by that Kamal..."

"Well yes."

"And the constant do-this-this-way and do-that-that-way...I mean it's just a takeaway, not the Hilton, for Christ's sake." She slid a Dove soap into the second bag.

"Yes, but Kamal is not there all the time," I said.

"I do miss Tarzan's stories though – never knew Bangladesh was a place till I met him, I thought it was just a bit in India that George Harrison sung about."

I looked at Wendy's thin face covered in pancake makeup. She wasn't young, probably old enough to buy a George Harrison single when it first came out. She stared into the distance. "Maybe I'm not a curry person."

I wasn't either, but with an electric bill the size of the rugby club carry-out and no one to help pay it, I had no choice. I either spent my nights switching everything on and off or served curries until something better came along.

I watched Wendy slide a slip of straw-coloured hair behind her ear. The rest was scraped into a tight bun, as immovable as my grocery through the checkout. Wendy was now in slow motion, lost in thought and oblivious to the queue forming behind me.

"But even if I was a curry person," said Wendy, "I still wouldn't want it for my wedding."

"Well we are all different," I said, now handing her things.

"That's what Fanny says."

"Fanny?"

"Everyone knows Fanny," she said.

I tied up a bag as Tenzam liked it... "Never met the woman," I muttered.

"Can you hurry up," said the pensioner behind me.

"She grew up here," said Wendy.

I handed her Tenzam's electric token with an "I need to go" stance.

"She massages the Rugby team," said Wendy, pushing Tenzam's electric token in the machine. "Sorted a few backs out I can tell you."

"So I have heard."

"A real miracle worker?" muttered the pensioner.

Wendy glared at the pensioner. "She runs a health business in Glasgow. Built it from nothing, while single-handedly bringing up her two kids..."

"Could you hurry up? The takeaway is opening," I said.

"...who are both doing absolutely marvellous at school."

"Yes, and I'm not getting any younger," said the pensioner.

"That Fanny has done well for herself," said Wendy, ignoring both me and the pensioner. "She's so successful she has a cleaner and two cars. She even earned enough to pay off her ex-husband without selling the house."

I watched the pensioner move to another checkout and the rest of the queue follow. I was beginning to hate this Fanny and I didn't even know what she looked like.

"I mean she's different to Mavis," Wendy said, leaning towards me. "They never got on, you know.

"That'll be Mavis from the post office," shouted the pensioner, "she never keeps you waiting."

I didn't want to hear any more and made a grab for the bags.

Wendy held on to the electric token. "I was surprised when Fanny said she was going to sort Mavis's wedding out."

"I am sure Mavis is quite capable of..."

"Still, if anyone can fix Mavis's wedding Fanny can. I mean Mavis is nice and all, but curry, in the community centre?"

"It could work," I muttered.

"Yes, so would a burger on 'the green,' but I wouldn't want that for a wedding either," muttered Wendy.

"Just off to the post office now – won't be long in there," said the pensioner, lifting her bags from the checkout.

"Well it's just as well we are not all the same then," I said, snatching the token. I made for the exit with a bristling walk.

"Tell Mavis I was asking after her," Wendy shouted.

"Aye, me too," shouted the cashier next to Wendy.

I kept on walking. Now I understood why Wendy's husband lingered at the Taj.

I headed full speed to the takeaway; it was five o'clock on Friday night and the Taj Mahal was always busy. As I crossed the road, I wondered if this was how all great artists lived... running errands for Bangladesh chefs, while living off staff curries full of bones which kept everything way too regular. Then I remembered I was no longer a great artist. And damn it – Wendy's husband would be there, killing time with talk of cricket, and worse still... Mavis had promised to "pop in" with more "Fanny and the wedding" news.

Chapter Thirteen

THE PANIC

You are never too old for sibling rivalry.

According to Mavis, Fanny is a sister no woman would want. She is ten years younger with a confidence that never wavers and a mother who believes in her 110 percent. And now, thanks to the whole Birthday Dad incident, Mavis talks of little else. She seems obsessed with Fanny, and it has come as quite a shock.

Mavis had always been the sort of woman who made the most of things. Sure, we had had our differences, but she seemed to me to be a strong, robust sort of woman who was happy to hold her own corner with anyone. We had performed many times together and she was always the first to give any heckler a mouthful. She took snatch from no one and didn't care what people thought of her.

Until Fanny came on the scene. Now Mavis seemed flustered and needy. I had never seen her like this before. To be honest, I had no idea how to help.

I left the co-op and, like a coward, walked the back road to the takeaway – avoiding the post office. Mavis would be closing up and loitering around the closed sign "looking out for me," and I couldn't face it. Besides, I told myself, it was a Friday night, the busiest night of the week – I really needed to get back.

Wendy's husband was already in the takeaway, and on his second beer. He along with the Roadworks Man were staring at the cricket in silent masculine bliss when Mavis entered, red-faced and emotional. I said nothing as she expertly skipped from the door as it crashed shy of her heels.

I answered the phone. "Taj Mahal."

Mavis began to mutter about her sister.

I motioned to Mavis that I was on the phone.

Mavis slumped in a chair next to the two men and pulled out her phone. Wendy's husband took one look at Mavis, downed his beer, and left.

"My sister is driving me crazy," she muttered.

"Sisters," said the Roadworks Man, staring at the TV.

"She wants to give me away," said Mavis. "Can you believe it? I haven't even asked her to the wedding."

The Roadworks Man nodded.

"I mean what am I, chopped liver?

The Roadworks Man pulled a face.

"Don't I have a say?"

"Weddings," tutted the Roadworks Man.

"She says mum's all for it."

"You have a mother?" said the Roadworks Man.

"She's in a home," I muttered with my hand over the phone.

"It's a given, she says – what the hell does that mean?" said Mavis.

"You never mentioned your mother before," said the Roadworks Man.

Mavis sighed. "She's in another world. Stares out the window and talks about her school days. Occasionally she returns to the present just long enough to make a sarcastic comment. Visiting her..."

"Requires alcohol," I muttered.

Mavis looked at me.

The Roadworks Man whistled through his teeth. "I never knew."

"I don't need giving away," muttered Mavis. "I'm perfectly capable of walking from one spot to the other."

The Roadworks Man pushed a poppadum across to Mavis.

Mavis didn't notice. Instead she flicked through her texts, ranting about Fanny's stupid "mini Taj Mahal" suggestion, "which Lumpy absolutely loved."

The Roadworks Man turned off the TV and looked at Mavis. "You have a sister called Fanny? What kind of woman answers to a name like that?"

Mavis looked up. "That's what Lumpy said – until he met her. Now he can't get enough of her, loves her ideas, don't know what he sees in her."

Betty walked in. The door snipped at her heels and she glared at it.

The Roadworks Man chuckled.

"I mean she even suggested a pig's head made of tofu," said Mavis. "For the banquet."

"Pig's head?" said Betty.

"Disgusting," mocked the Roadworks Man, and then shouted at Tenzam, asking him what would he do with a tofu pig.

Tenzam didn't understand, I could tell. "Just coming," he shouted, turning off his Bollywood music.

"Although Lumpy says it's a joke," said Mavis. "Do you see me laughing?"

"I can't remember the last time I saw you laugh," said Betty. "You should spend some time with Amanda, she'd cheer you up."

Amanda was the new bookshop owner. Betty had spent the afternoon with her, which according to Betty was "absolutely fabulous."

"She's a hoot," said Betty, "you should meet her."

The last person I wanted to hear about, let alone meet, was Amanda. I had loved that shop and working in it. Since it had been taken over, I tried hard not to think about it and never walked past it. Unlike Betty, who walked past it every day – then updated me on any changes. Reading body language was never her thing.

"That Amanda is something else," said Betty and gave me an order a mile long. I began to write it down.

"She ushered me in like a long-lost buddy," said Betty. "Even though they weren't open. That's Americans for you, so accommodating."

I scribbled over the mess of an order and rewrote it.

"She made me coffee just how you make it," Betty looked at me. "And the shop is awesome."

"Really. "I muttered.

I screwed up the now complete mess of an order and wrote another.

"Amanda's organising an open day for the bookshop," said Betty.

"So I've heard," said the Roadworks Man.

"She's selling raffle tickets, for the pipe band," said Betty.

"Pipe band," said the Roadworks Man, "what's that got to do with a bookshop?"

"Exactly," I said.

"Oh, it's all about heritage," said Betty. "She's into it; she has a whole shelf on roots and things."

"Roots? What's that to do with a pipe band," said the Roadworks Man.

I tossed the screwed paper in the bin and realised I tossed both in, pulled out both, flattened out the wrong one, and handed it to Tenzam, who had appeared beside me.

"Amanda likes korma," said Tenzam, "and coconut rice."

I glared at him. "I thought you said korma is not a real curry."

Tenzam smiled at Betty and she laughed.

Betty, like most women, mothered him. She even left some of her husband's clothes for him. The hand-me-downs swamped Tenzam's five-foot-two frame, making him look even younger and increased his "tipping" appeal. Some weeks he made more in tips than my wage…

"This Amanda, she leaves tips too." He glanced at me. "Good tips."

Betty chuckled. "First prize is a hot tub."

"Hot tub?" said the Roadworks Man. "Here in Lochgilphead?"

"You could win." Betty looked at me. "Imagine that. You and the Bag Lady wouldn't be fighting over your naans anymore."

"Hot tub – what the hell has that got to do with a bookshop or a pipe band," said the Roadworks Man.

Tenzam took the correct order from me and flashed another smile at Betty. "Extra sauce and no ghee, just how you like it."

I threw him my typical "over-egging it again" glare.

"I'd love a hot tub," said Betty. She looked at Mavis. "Wouldn't you?"

Mavis looked at Betty. "My sister has one."

"Awesome," muttered Betty.

"I'd prefer another job," I said, still looking at Tenzam.

The Roadworks Man eyed Betty's wiry eighty-year-old frame. She was misleadingly frail looking. Betty could out-walk anyone; she walked everywhere, especially in the rain. Betty loved the rain.

"What would you want with a hot tub?" he said, sucking on a wedge of lemon. He eyed her. "At your time of life?"

"And what time is that?" she said.

The Roadworks Man laughed as Betty squeezed herself into a chair beside him.

Mavis slipped her phone back into her pocket. "I can't believe Fanny Pain-in-the-Arse has joined forces with Lumpy."

The Roadworks Man let out a loud laugh. "When can I meet Miss Pain-in-the-Arse Fanny?"

"'Joining forces' is a bit strong," said Betty.

"He likes the Taj Mahal idea," said Mavis.

"That's Lumpy's for you – full of surprises," muttered the Roadworks Man.

Mavis glared at the Roadworks Man. "We are to sit on the floor."

"Lumpy said that was your idea," muttered the Roadworks Man.

"He did that," said Betty. "He said you'd like it – reminded you of your belly dancing dos."

The Roadworks Man laughed. "Could be worse – you could be having it in here."

He gestured to the seating area. One wall was covered by mirror tiles Blu-Tacked on and another with a cheesy painting of the Taj Mahal with two cartoon Indians doing a thumbs-up. The tables were covered in red paper tablecloths and so close together that anyone over a size sixteen took one look and ordered a takeaway.

We silently watched as Tenzam appeared, thumped the music player, which had been stuck on the same song, and returned to the kitchen.

"He has a point," said I.

"And," said the Roadworks Man, "your sister says it will make your mum happy..."

"Making my mum happy requires tablets," Mavis muttered.

Chapter Fourteen

THE RISE OF SAINT FANNY

Gossip is best listened to with enough alcohol not to care and enough not to remember.

Mavis followed me to Tesco's. The Taj Mahal had run out of tomatoes, and as Tesco's was the only place open, we headed there.

It was not one of my better ideas.

Jessie was standing by her car, absently waving at a passing car. She was glowing with happiness, in a bright blue and gold sari. Her red hair was scooped up into a stylish bun and her eyes darkened with kohl. She looked exotic, nothing like the beige daughter of Birthday Dad – and it seemed she was hell-bent on advertising it.

She waved at us, sending Mavis into a series of mutterings about "ignoring," "walk the other way," and "what the hell is that she's wearing?"

The last person she wanted to talk to was Jessie. In fact, she was as much up for Jessie and her "how great is Fanny" speech as she was for root canal treatment.

I couldn't blame her.

Jessie had spread it about that "Fanny charmed the pants off her dad and had "probably added a few weeks onto his life." Fanny finally visited Birthday Dad who, now claiming he was imprisoned, was refusing to eat or leave his bed. The Ban Duic incident left him in pain and shouting about it and he blamed the hospital staff.

"This place is infested with spies," he said.

Fanny, with a few finger presses in the right place and a good talking-to, had worked miracles. Not only was Birthday Dad pain free, but he was home again. After Fanny's visit, Birthday Dad had marched up and down the ward driving the staff insane. He threatened to catch the bus so many times the cleaner took him home and he hadn't marched since. Birthday Dad was now peaceful and, to quote Jessie, almost bearable for her mother.

To be honest, even I was sick of hearing about it.

I mean standing in the takeaway is bad enough, but when every second person who comes in goes on about St. Fanny, even I wanted to slap her. Suddenly the whole world and its dogs knew a woman I had never heard of before. But then, I guess I never worked in a takeaway with the Roadworks Man keeping me and every customer updated with every bit of gossip going.

"Hey girls," shouted Jessie, "great to see you." She beckoned us over. "Just want to tell you about your amazing Fanny."

"She is not my Fanny," said Mavis with a forced smile.

Jessie didn't hear; she had spotted another car and was madly waving, sending her bangles into a frenzy of jingling. "Congratulations, by the way," she said, "on the big day. Not easy at our age." She laughed.

"What?" said Mavis.

Jessie's hand fluttered about her face, pushing a strand of hair behind her ears. "And having Fanny must be a big help."

"Big help? My sister," said Mavis with a "get stuffed" stance, "thinks she knows what people want and doesn't need to ask..."

"Sisters who'd have 'em." I feigned a laugh. Then I noticed the chef sitting in Jessie's car, relaxed and looking almost appealing. He threw a wave at me and got out of the car.

"You remember these two," Jessie said to him.

"Yes, I remember," he said, pulling out a vapour cigarette. "The restaurant has never been the same since your dance."

Jessie laughed. "He hasn't touched a real one since the hospital."

"Who needs 'em," the chef said with almost a smile.

It was hard to tell if he was joking or not. Then Jessie without any prompting started to tell us how she loved helping out in Ban Duic and getting to wear all these Asian dresses.

"I feel like a new woman," she said. The chef beamed at Jessie.

I stared at her get-up and wanted to spit chips. Jessie was now happily doing what I fancied doing while I was doing what most people had refused to do. And she had transformed a grumpy cigarette-tossing chef into a happy non-smoker. I turned to Mavis, looking for some comfort, and there she was looking like a schoolgirl at Kamal as he sauntered up to the car. He slid a bag of onions into the back seat and smiled at her.

"The beautiful Mavis," he said. Mavis's face lit up – a first for months.

"Yes," said Jessie. "I often help out, don't I?" She looked at the chef.

"That you do," he said.

"Fanny has asked the chef for some ideas," said Jessie to Mavis. "Don't you worry, we'll save your wedding."

"Tenzam and Lumpy have it under control," I said. "Mavis wants a small and intimate affair."

"In the community centre?" said Jessie. "That place is about as intimate as a toilet with a broken lock. Fanny is your only hope."

"That's right, Fanny is an expert on everything," muttered Mavis.

"Everything?" said the chef.

"She has always been delusional. She has saved the world several times." Mavis looked at Kamal. "Didn't you know?"

Kamal looked confused.

"In fact," said Mavis, "none of us would be here without her."

"Imagine that," muttered Kamal.

"How does she save the world then?" said Jessie, unimpressed.

"Oh, on Facebook she signs petitions."

I was the only one to laugh, and mid cackle I spied Lumpy exiting Tesco's. He stood at the door and watched as Mavis finished her joke. I am not sure if he heard or not, but he looked from her to Kamal and didn't smile once. Instead, clutching a Tesco "forever bag," he walked over.

Mavis looked at Lumpy. "Did you phone? If you did, I didn't answer because it was switched off, my sister is doing my head in."

"Thought you'd like something plain," said Lumpy.

"Oh?"

"Yes, I thought we could make some of that soup you like."

"I see."

He glanced at Kamal. "Give the curry a miss?"

Mavis didn't say a word. Instead she looked in Lumpy's bag.

"Turnip and carrots," said Lumpy. "Grated?"

"Yum."

"And cheese in the scones."

Mavis smiled. "Absolutely."

"And I will make extra for your mum," said Lumpy, steering Mavis away.

I didn't hear the rest except for a small laugh from Mavis as Lumpy opened the car door.

Chapter Fifteen

THE MEASURING TAPE

There is more to karma than joss sticks.

That night as I went home I saw the Bag Lady and Betty huddled over the fire talking like they were plotting something illegal. They were engrossed and didn't notice me until the wind slammed the gate shut.

Betty jumped.

"What are you up to?" I said.

"Nothing," said the Bag Lady, shoving a paper up her sleeve.

"Nothing?" I said.

"Yes, nothing..."

"Funny kind of nothing," I muttered.

"Well the fire is out and we are just wondering about calling it a night," said Betty.

"Bit early?" I said.

"Shifty wants me back." Betty sniffed. "He'll be here any minute."

"And what about the bhuna?" I gestured to the takeaway.

"He's made me steak tartare."

"Again?"

"Apparently it's full of iron – which for an ol' bird..." She poked at the remains of the fire. "So he says."

I went inside. I hated it when Shifty came to pick his mother up;

he was always nippy with me, like it was my fault his mother preferred takeaway in my garden to his posh grub in his "bespoke" hotel.

Once he did try his hand at a few Asian dishes; Betty after one mouthful called it a poor man's ragu and gave it to Bingo, Shifty's dog, who didn't even sniff it let alone eat it.

I opened my curry and stared out of the kitchen window. I could just make them out under the fading sunset. They were whispering to each other – something about the shed – and then Betty pulled a small box from her bag.

I put on my glasses and saw it was a builder's tape measure...

The Bag Lady began to pull the tape from it. I watched as the thin strip caught the moonlight with a bounce.

"Careful, she'll see us," whispered the Bag Lady as Betty gestured her to backtrack to the corner of the shed.

The Bag Lady whispered a few numbers as she moved to different points near the shed while Betty wrote on her hand.

"Just one more," the Bag Lady whispered.

"This time let's imagine it with the shed out of the way," said Betty.

I flicked the patio light on; they stopped like two cats caught mid pounce.

"What are you two up to," I shouted.

No one heard. Shifty's powder-blue mini reversed up the drive with a dramatic skid on the gravel. It was a car no one could ignore. It had "Critters for Sniggers" written on the sides in psychedelic writing surrounded by bright-coloured sixties flowers. Shifty had gotten it for a song, and now, having fallen in love with the deco, he couldn't face spray-painting Argyll Hotel over the top of it.

Shifty let off a few "I'm in no mood for waiting" revs, then jumped out of the car with a door slam.

I watched Shifty head towards his mother with a look no mother would want to see – apart from Betty. She relished annoying her son. Betty had spent a lifetime battling her husband, and now that he was gone, she had no intentions of pleasing a son who, according to her, was "turning into his father."

Betty pressed the rewind button – the tape flicked back and Shifty grabbed it off her.

"What are you doing with this? It's mine!"

"I like things dimensional," said Betty.

"Dimensional?"

"Yes, and thinking outside by the trees."

Shifty let out a sigh. "What has that got to do with the price of fish?"

"Fish?" said Betty with a coquettish smile.

"We're just measuring things," said the Bag Lady.

"What? Why? Actually, you know what, I don't care," said Shifty, "just give me my tape measure and come home."

"We are nearly finished," said the Bag Lady.

"I am fed up with your nonsense – you are as bad as that Jessica's dad. Perhaps we should get the doctor to test you again."

"We are making room for pondering," Betty said, still looking impish.

"That's ridiculous, you can ponder anywhere," snapped Shifty.

"How can I ponder in that place, with you and my dead husband roaming around?" said Betty.

"That place is your place."

"Not anymore."

"And dead people do not roam there," said Shifty.

"That's what you say," said Betty. She turned to the Bag Lady. "I feel liberated here."

"Liberated? What the hell are you talking about?"

"Liberation at my age doesn't come often."

"Liberation from what, the Cold War?"

"You can be a bit bossy," muttered the Bag Lady.

"I like to look at the stars" – Betty gestured to the sky – "and imagine up there somewhere is where your father will eventually go..." She threw a loony look at her son. "To fight the powers that be and lose."

Shifty pulled a childish "I'm not listening" face.

"When he's done haunting that is..." Betty smiled.

"Mother, you're talking rubbish again ."

"And I am not going to get that sitting in the Argyll feeding Bingo your ragu, am I?"

Shifty picked up her bag. "Jesus."

Betty began to waffle about the afterlife and how her husband was trapped in the hotel. And before Shifty had a chance to interrupt, she moved onto meditation, karma, and the Book of the Dying Dead. "Or is it the Dead of Dying?" she muttered.

Shifty looked at her with a blank face.

She matched his stare.

He sighed. "Come on Mum, it's time for home."

Betty ignored him and turned to the Bag Lady. "I like to think that karma has caught up with him, while I am sitting by this fire drinking tea."

"That's not tea, Mother, I can smell it off you."

"He is regretting things – through gritted teeth." She looked at her son. "If ghosts have teeth that is."

"Some would say that sort of thinking would cause a dead man harm," said the Bag Lady.

Shifty handed Betty her jacket; she waved him away.

"I know," said Betty, "ain't it great?"

Shifty rolled his eyes. "What the hell are you talking about?"

"But that is not the point – if you want peace, you have to forgive," said the Bag Lady. "Let the poor bugger go."

"Where is the fun in that? I want revenge."

The Bag Lady shook her head.

"Angry feels good – it makes me feel alive."

"Hot tea does it for me," muttered the Bag Lady.

"I am still here," snapped Shifty.

Chapter Sixteen

THE SECRET

Revenge is like chocolate – too much leads to indigestion.

After Betty left, the Bag Lady retreated into her teepee. Puss, appearing from nowhere, meowed outside until, with a grunt, the Bag Lady unzipped her tent and let her in.

How things had changed...

Before the Bag Lady moved into my garden it was a tidy space with a neat garden and a shed that Rodger hid in. No one sat in it; even Puss skipped across the grass to somewhere better, until the Bag Lady erected her teepee. She built campfires, burnt things, and collected junk from her walks. And my garden turned into a meeting place full of artistically arranged rubbish where women whinged, laughed, and drank by the fire.

I soon stopped watching TV.

Originally the Bag Lady lived in a small one-man tepee that you couldn't even flip a pancake in, and she decorated it with the junk she collected. She had sheep skulls swinging from various points on the roof, an old bath mat for a welcome mat – except no one was welcome inside, apart from Puss – and a collection of shells tied together that clattered in the breeze.

She was happy enough until one day a wind the speed of a juggernaut blew the teepee across the yard and beyond, the bath mat into the canal, and her skulls across several gardens, causing just as many complaints.

Betty, who was by now her bosom buddy, organised a "whip-around" at the Argyll and a bigger teepee was sourced with a small wood-burning stove. Sheryl brought her a proper outdoor impossible-to-blow-away mat with No Men Allowed scrawled across it. And an agreement was reached: any skulls and the like collected were to be kept inside the teepee.

Betty had wangled her way into the new tent while the junk soon wangled its way outside again. Betty even helped the Bag Lady with her arrangements, nailing skulls onto trees so they were windproof and painting the shells with glitter, until the Bag Lady told her to stop.

Betty had a way of doing things with a flounce and a dusting-off with her hands. Watching her toss wood onto the fire was like watching a six-year-old toss a pancake. Which was more than misleading because Betty could implant a nail in the toughest of wood. Unlike the Bag Lady, who wielded a hammer like a shot-putter and thumped everything into oblivion.

They were an odd pair who soon became inseparable, but never secretive – until now.

I wondered what women their age had to be so secretive about. But then the Bag Lady and Betty weren't like other women. And I had no idea what their ages were except that they were eligible for a free bus pass.

I told Mavis about the measuring tape.

"I have never seen either of them use a measuring tape, even when they hung that swing from a tree," I said. "What do you think they are up to?"

Mavis didn't even flutter an eyelash.

"Who cares," she said. "I have a potential wedding disaster on my hands. I have enough to think about."

I told Mavis she was becoming self-obsessed.

And she, after a "pot-kettle-black," comment, said, "What bride-to-be isn't?"

She did have a point, although I had no intentions of telling her.

Instead I watched Betty and the Bag Lady over the next few days. They had started to spend time away from the tent.

And I decided to follow...

Not a hard thing to do in Lochgilphead. It's so small you can walk around on your tea break and so quiet you can cross the road with your eyes closed – cats sleep on the road, it's that dead.

A few days later, after half an hour of loitering, I spotted them in the bookshop. It was the last place I would want to look. I finally steeled myself to walk down the street on the opposite side. There behind the "Closed" sign stood the two of them talking with Amanda – like grown-ups at a parent–teacher meeting. Albeit the Bag Lady was dressed like a bag lady, and Betty was dressed like she was ready to scale "Mount Whatever" in a hurricane.

Betty was in her uniform of walking boots, waterproofs, and hat of choice, today's being an expensive hat of aqua blue, revealing a woman of means who coordinates.

The aqua-blue hat matched her nails, which she flashed with her usual flamboyant gestures. Betty's hands had a life of their own. The Bag Lady called them her Italian hands and said she couldn't speak without them. And, as I stared across the street, they were working overtime in the bookshop.

They saw me watching from across the road and waved. Suddenly I wished I had something better to do. I waved back with my best "I'm just on my way to somewhere important" face.

Amanda opened the door and shouted me in.

"What do you think?" said Amanda. Her pixie face crinkled into a smile. She was a tiny woman with a fondness for expensive, earthy clothes, which she bought from a "petite" online store.

I stared at the bookshop. It was chaotic and busy. The shelves had been ripped out, the walls were covered with wet patches of plaster, and there were boxes everywhere, one opened and overflowing with posters. In the middle of the floor was a sleek, computerised till with instructions scattered around it, and in the corner was a coffee machine filling the room with an aroma that had my mouth watering.

Amanda grabbed a poster and unrolled it.

I stared at the till. It was the sort of till I would have given my anything for in the takeaway.

Amanda rattled the poster in front of me with an "isn't it wonderful" look. "Betty and the Bag Lady helped me design it," she said.

It was orange in many shades. Splashed across the top, large and bold, was the heading "Open Day at the Book Centre" with "Come sniff out a story" in orange underneath.

All of which led the eye to a comic drawing of Amanda, peering over a *Scottish Secrets* book, wearing librarian glasses and a cryptic smile.

"I'm calling this" – she gestured to the empty walls – "The Book Centre, 'shop' is so passé."

I ran my fingers over the till. It was everything you would want, and nothing like the rubbish till in the takeaway – which had to be prised open with a screwdriver.

"The Argyll has one of these," I muttered. "It does everything."

"Apart from coffee," laughed Amanda.

"The shop is going to be orange," said Betty.

"Orange? For a bookshop?" I said.

"Yes, with shelving from IKEA," said the Bag Lady.

I looked around the shop. What the hell did the Bag Lady know about IKEA?

"Cappuccino," said Betty, poised at the machine, with one of her Italian hand gestures.

"Black," I muttered, pushing the tray of the till in and out – it glided like a bird across the water.

The tray was empty except for an envelope with a five-figure number and "to beat" written underneath in capital letters.

I looked at Amanda.

"That," she said, "is the record we are going to smash into oblivion."

Chapter Seventeen

THE RAFFLE

Raffles are as much fun as driving in the rain without a windscreen wiper.

The Bag Lady and Betty were Amanda's "happy helpers" who seemed to know an awful lot about "reading centres."

I watched the Bag Lady talk about the importance of shelving like she ran a library. Why did she care? She'd always been a reclusive person.

"I am all ears," laughed Amanda. As the Bag Lady moved on to my shop, calling it the "old shop," which as she put it did not "utilise shelving properly."

"You need to surprise people," said the Bag Lady. "Be unpredictable, that's what I used to say to her" – the Bag Lady waved her hand at me – "but would she listen?"

I threw the Bag Lady a glare as Betty handed me one of the best black coffees I had ever tasted.

"It's all about timing," said Betty.

I sipped the coffee; the bittersweet taste trickled down to my stomach.

"Yes, you can sell more raffle tickets at a do than anywhere," said Betty. "Trust me, the Argyll practically ran on raffle tickets when I owned it."

I looked at the Bag Lady.

The Argyll was almost bankrupt when Betty and her husband owned it. I waited for one of the Bag Lady's scratchy comments. She smiled with a nod.

What had happened to these two women? They actually seemed focused and knew what they were talking about. They talked about fundraising like it was a piece of cake.

"What's the fascination with raffles?" I said.

"Oh, they're taking over the raffle," said Amanda. "Which is such a big help. My husband was going to, but..." She looked away. "He's busy, won't be here on time. And now they have come up with this idea to break the record for the most raffle tickets sold in Argyll. And this is the figure they have to beat."

Amanda slapped the "figure to beat" envelope on top of her "top of the range" bright blue funky till with a chunk of Blu-Tack.

"I had no idea there was such a thing," she laughed.

"Everyone's got a till like that," I said, "apart from the takeaway."

"No, sweetheart, I meant the record."

Over the next few weeks, Betty and the Bag Lady took up the challenge with as much gusto as they did for erecting their fires. They were everywhere – the co-op, the library, the Argyll – rattling a bucket full of coins and jabbing raffle tickets at passers-by. They even had their photo on the *Fyne News* and the book centre's Facebook page.

And I hardly saw them. During the day they were out, and at night they were in the tent with it firmly zipped closed. Only Puss, after a decent amount of meowing, was allowed in.

For the first time since the Bag Lady had moved into my garden, it was silent, apart from the distant babbling of a burn and Puss meowing at the tent.

I actually looked forward to 4.30 when I could go to the takeaway. And then dreaded coming home, sitting in the kitchen and staring out onto a closed tent with a glass of whatever for one.

Chapter Eighteen

CHINESE TAKEAWAY

There are reasons couples fight that even they are unaware of.

avis spent another night on the couch, and this time Lumpy didn't call.

The night before, they had arrived at the Taj Mahal holding hands. They were on their way to picking up Chinese and had popped in to see if I would like to join them after I finished work.

Thanks to a four-figure order of a rugby club portion, I had just finished a delivery. I had been out in the rain risking the first decent haircut I had had in months in a street where the houses were numbered as randomly as a set of lottery balls. I searched for a whole hour for a house which had no number and no lights to show that there was no number. I had knocked on five doors, been sniffed, pawed, and then barked at by a dribbling dog and proposition by a man so thin that I am sure, if I had taken him up on his offer, he would not have survived a kiss let alone anything else.

"A woman like you shouldn't be out in the rain," he said, thrusting his unshaven chin forward, "have a dram, and I'll warm you up" – which was as inviting as a day in A&E.

Finally, the takeaway was delivered to a drunk who left me standing in the rain while she "searched for her purse" with the aid of a distant male voice.

"It's in the drawer."

"Which drawer?"

"The kitchen drawer."

"Can you not get it?"

"The News is on."

"I can't find it, you've been in these drawers."

"I never touch your frigging drawers."

"Well someone's been at them."

It took ages for her to find her purse. And then when she did, she proceeded to count out her money like a dyslexic miser.

"Ten, eleven, twelve, twenty..."

"Thirteen" (Me).

"Sorry thirteen, fourteen...is that a tenner?"

"No – a fiver" (Me).

While I stood in a monsoon downpour.

I arrived back at the restaurant drenched and pissed.

I crashed through the restaurant door – which clipped my heels – staggered, tripped, and dumped the empty food box on the counter.

"Have a good trip?" said the Roadworks Man without looking up from his paper.

"Hardly," I snapped.

"Lumpy's swinging by later," he said, "wants to know if you're up for a Chinese."

I looked at him. "Lumpy's doing Chinese?"

"Mavis," muttered the Roadworks Man.

"I see," I said.

"The mother's not doing too well," he said, "and he's trying to cheer her up with a no-spice treat."

I answered the phone when it rang...it was Kamal, the boss, with another delivery.

Kamal is a man who has no understanding of the word "no." His tactic is seduction, confusion, and then intimidation, always when you least expect it. Kamal's delicious smile, seductive voice, and then the "dare you to say no" bark all served to catch you off guard. And he was always catching me when I was unprepared and rushed off my feet.

The restaurant phone was connected to his phone. If Tenzam or I didn't answer it within one ring, then he did, and he always said yes to a delivery, no matter where it was. Making a running dive for the phone before he answered it was our only option – not easy when you just tripped in the door.

Tonight was no different.

"You told me we don't do deliveries," I said on the phone. *Like I said every night.*

"Any orders over fifty we do." *Like he said every night.*

"When was that decided?" I said.

Kamal began to breathe heavily. "This delivery is important and it's only five minutes away."

"You said that about the last one."

"I didn't tell you to walk."

"I'll stay until you're back," said the Roadworks Man with a casual flick of his paper.

"But you stay anyway," I snapped.

Lumpy and Mavis arrived holding hands. I waved a hello.

"This order always tips," said Kamal.

"That's what you said last time."

"Of course, the tip is yours," he snapped and hung up.

Tenzam tentatively placed the order on the bench. "Thank you," he said. "It is a big help to us."

I picked up the box.

He looked at me with his big brown eyes and smiled. And I melted; with one sentence, he had me liking him, feeling sorry for him, saying yes – until I saw the address, and then I wanted to curse him.

"It's your friend the bookshop lady," said Tenzam.

"She is not a friend," I muttered.

"And she always tips big."

I had heard that one before...

I drove out into the dark, with directions from the Roadworks Man and Lumpy, who had both assured me it was a "piece of cake to find."

"It's just by that red phone box which doesn't work," said the Road-works Man.

"Which phone box?" I said.

"Just ignore the dog," said the Roadworks Man, still engrossed in his paper, "it barks at anything."

"What?"

"And you're best to reverse in to the drive," said Lumpy, "it's a blind corner."

"Blind corner?"

"Oh, Lumpy's a dream with blind corners," said Mavis with a paternal pat on his hand.

"But mind the boat by the drive," said the Roadworks Man.

"Which you won't see in the dark unless you hit it," said Lumpy.

"Thanks," I muttered.

"And I'll be here when you get back," Mavis reassured me, presumably with the Chinese.

Amanda's house was lit up with solar lights glistening in the rain. I stood under her porch with a grateful sigh as the monsoon retreated to a drizzle. I looked around. Her porch was empty apart from a selection of wind chimes.

Her garden was empty too; it was a complete, uncluttered Zen experience of rocks and sand. I knocked with the yin-and-yang door knocker, knocked on the window, yelled through the letterbox, and finally rattled a smiling fat Buddha wind chime.

"Just coming..." she shouted.

I waited and wondered what a week with the Bag Lady and her skull collection would do to Amanda's garden.

"Sorry, can't find a thing in this place." She laughed and opened the door in her dressing gown and a makeup-less face. She flashed a smile and greeted me like a long-lost friend.

"Come in while I find my purse," she said.

I stood in the hallway, empty apart from a pair of flowery wellies.

She told me to go into the lounge and take a seat; it too was empty. I wondered if she had taken the whole Zen thing too far.

She gestured to a large box. "Won't be long, do you want some tea? It'll have to be black, forgot the milk." She paused. "He was going to bring it."

She disappeared and began to shout from another room about "late trains"; "changed plans"; how "these things happen" and "thank God for the Bag Lady and Betty."

Amanda was living out of a suitcase, with two saucepans and a kettle from Oxfam. Everything from her other home was stuck on an island in the Atlantic. There had been a "cock-up" with the addresses and her husband, who was supposed to arrive three hours ago, was still at their old home trying to sort things out.

"Why he can't sort things out here is beyond me," she said, appearing with a purse under her arm and two mugs.

"Lapsang souchong?"

Amanda looked the sort that not only didn't use a teabag but never used dairy either.

"Don't know when he's coming now," she said.

I looked at the huge carry-out.

She laughed feebly. "Guess I have to freeze some of this." She looked around. "If I had one..." She caught my eye. "Do you have one?" I looked at her. "I mean could you put some of it in your freezer just until mine arrives?"

She opened the takeaway and began to rummage, divided the boxes into two, and then rearranged them, muttering to herself more than me.

"He sent me ahead to organise things." She sighed. "Now I have to do the whole opening day on my own. At least I've got those two to help."

She stopped and caught her breath. "There is so much food."

We both looked at the two piles of food.

"Why don't you just give it to the Bag Lady and her nice friend? They're such gems."

❄

I arrived back to find no Mavis and no Lumpy, just Tenzam and the Roadworks man looking grim and Kamal in the kitchen having an argument with the gas cooker.

There had been a rush of two people. Kamal, clearing away the plates, tripped over the Roadworks Man's jacket and Lumpy laughed.

Tripping for Kamal was a capital offence, let alone being laughed at. Mavis tried to soothe the situation, which seemed to rile Lumpy, and the hand-holding abruptly stopped. Finally – from nowhere, a dispute erupted over the wedding cake.

"Cake?" I said.

"Let's just say that Lumpy's idea of a cake and Kamal's are different," said the Roadworks man.

"I see," I said.

"She's gone to your place."

Chapter Nineteen

THE PRODIGY

"There is a spice for every occasion, but not every occasion requires spice."

The house was in darkness when I arrived home. I walked into the kitchen, dumped Amanda's takeaway on the bench, and switched on the kettle.

I was staring at my empty freezer, wondering who had eaten all the bread, when Mavis came in. I listened to her plod about the kitchen like she had no idea where the tea was.

"Aren't you worried?" I said. "I mean how many times can a couple fall out?"

She laughed and muttered about "wedding nerves" but I could tell she was tense; she was opening and shutting each cupboard and staring.

I told her to sit down, that I would make the tea, but she didn't listen and continued to look.

"The tea is in the same place," I said.

She ignored me and carried on... I gave up and took a seat.

"All's I said was that Kamal had a point" – she let out a nervous cough – "and he says I am taking sides."

"Kamal had a point? Since when?"

Mavis finally stopped at the tea cupboard and stared at my herbal collection like she'd never seen the packets before.

"Since he said Tenzam's ideas were stupid."

"Kamal calls Tenzam stupid all the time."

"Tenzam had this idea about the cake."

"You having cake now? I thought you had decided…"

"Yes, well my sister says a wedding without a cake is like a massage without oil. And as I apparently have no idea about cake, she'd organise one."

"What about the Women's Guild ?"

"She sorted them out."

"She sorted the Woman's Guild out – how is that possible? Those women intimidate Kamal."

"She came up with this ridiculous idea of a broom sitting on top of a postbox-shaped cake. And they told her to stuff it."

"The Women's Guild would never say 'stuff it.'"

"With me waving out of the postbox, and Lumpy on top sweeping the broom. 'It will be a hoot,' says Fanny."

"A broom and postbox in fondant, that'll not come cheap," I said.

Mavis pulled out a mint box, turned it in her hand, and put it back. "That's what Kamal said. Lumpy and the Roadworks Man laughed their heads off…"

"So, he has a sense of humour."

Mavis looked at me. "But that's not like him. He's usually sensitive, especially when it comes to my sister; he knows how I feel."

"I didn't even know you had one until…"

Mavis flicked the kettle on with vengeance. "My sister the prodigy, always making up ridiculous ideas. And when they didn't work she'd tell everyone they were my idea. Mum of course would believe her, not me. Like that stupid mini Taj Mahal. Fanny will probably try and make it eatable or something even more insane and then blame me when someone gets food poison." Mavis finally pulled a teabag from a box. "Kamal calls it an insult."

"Everything insults Kamal; he even gets offended when the gas cooker packs up. And he got that off eBay – I mean what does he expect."

"Fanny says a mini Taj would be great for the children."

"You mean like a bouncy castle? Your sister wants you have a bouncy castle at your wedding? Where's the romance in that?"

"That's what Kamal said." Mavis sighed.

"Then Lumpy said at our age romance is pain-free sex, and he polished it off with the Deep Heat joke. I think he was pissed off by then, he was throwing dirty looks at Kamal."

"No one laughs at that Deep Heat joke; well, apart from the Road-works Man."

"Kamal called that an insult and all."

She flicked the kettle on again and began a search for mugs. I was beginning to wonder if she actually remembered being in my kitchen at all.

"And then she rings up, on Lumpy's phone. I asked Lumpy what she was doing with his number. He didn't answer. 'She says that she has a red thing for you,' shouts Lumpy across the restaurant like everyone should hear. 'What is this, a garage sale for Orphan Annie?' I said, and do you know what Lumpy did?"

Mavis finally sat down.

"Nothing," she paused; "absolutely nothing. So I told him I'm wearing yellow – like Sheryl. Then Lumpy makes some Charlie Dimmock joke."

(Lumpy often compared Sheryl to Charlie Dimmock, a voluptuous gardener on TV.)

"Kamal asked who Charlie Dimmock was." Mavis almost smiled. "And when I told him, do you know what he said? 'You look nothing like a gardener.'"

"Typical," I said. "Kamal can be a real sleaze."

Mavis carried on...

"'Neither does Charlie Dimmock,' says Lumpy. Who then said I was 'more a Betty White than Charlie Dimmock.' Then Kamal asked me who Betty White was and I told him that she was an eighty-year-old comedian with very tight white hair. 'Aye but she wasn't always eighty,' said Lumpy and laughed again."

Mavis slumped in her chair.

"I don't know what's happening to us. Lumpy says I don't laugh anymore, but what is there to laugh at?"

I looked at Mavis's sad face. Lumpy had told me that Mavis's mother was in a bad way and didn't have long. I asked her about her mother. She fingered her engagement ring.

"Kamal says I'm not a red person, that I am more purple and blue."

"Typical," I said.

"I mean why is Fanny bothering just now?" said Mavis. "With everything else that is going on?"

I looked at Mavis; her eyes were full of tears. I didn't have the heart to ask about Tenzam's ideas for the cake again, let alone her mother. Instead I shoved the curry in the freezer, pulled out a packet of crisps, and poured us both a drink.

Chapter Twenty

THE SPICE RACK

Not all spices are "spicy".

The next day, I opened the door to a sheepish-looking Lumpy peering inside for any signs of his woman. He said he was feeling bad about the night before.

Tenzam had come up with the idea of a cardamom and spice pudding instead of cake, and Lumpy thought it was a wonderful idea until he told Mavis.

"It's not easy for her at the moment," he muttered. "I think I was a little flippant."

Mavis was on the couch pretending to be asleep.

"We're not having a cake or pudding," he shouted to the lounge room.

Mavis feigned a snore.

"Tenzam's had another idea," he shouted.

Mavis snored louder.

I told Lumpy to go in.

The Bag Lady and Betty were outside at the time. They had come back early from their adventures and were ecstatic. They had broken the raffle record and decided to honour this spectacular moment by buying a couple of scratch cards.

"We have won," Betty shouted, tapping on the patio door. "Ten pounds and it is only the beginning."

Mavis slept through the whole thing.

Ten pounds, apparently, was a sign that things were on the up for the two. And the two of them had decided on a bonfire to end all bonfires – a bonfire of celebrations, along with a few spicy kebabs.

The Bag Lady had an idea for tofu on a stick, flamed, smoked, and grilled, with a variety of spicy oils liberally applied.

Lumpy and I watched from the kitchen while Mavis "got herself ready."

Betty, in a festive mood, was in and out of the kitchen spreading barbecue joy like an excited six-year-old helping her dad.

"You have any of that nice mint dip left?"

"Where's the paper plates?"

"She's wanting more oil, some of that spicy stuff," she said.

Mavis let out a loud cough.

"It'll go well with the kebabs," said Betty, spying a bottle of Diet Coke in the fridge. "We could do with some of that – think there's a bit of vodka in the tent."

"You have vodka in the tent."

"Only for pondering," Betty laughed and skipped out.

Watching Betty skip was a sight I couldn't help but admire. And watching the Bag Lady lasso wood from the back of the garden, hack it up with an axe, and then construct a neat, never-to-fall-down bonfire kept both me and Lumpy entertained all morning. My garden was alive again, and getting a good tidy-up.

"Women but not as we know it," said Lumpy.

I laughed...

The fire was difficult to start; there had been a downpour and the wood was damp. Betty was in three times for firelighters and finally went into the shed for dryer junk to burn.

I offered Lumpy another coffee, making jokes about cooking kebabs in the kitchen. "It'll be Christmas before they get that beast lit," I said as I began to fill up the kettle.

I was feeling at peace with the world. My garden was full of people again, Puss was out and about watching, and Mavis had started to hum.

Then I saw from the corner of my eye Betty throw a couple of old cushions on the fire, along with a bottle of something.

"Lumpy," I said, "where did those cushions come from?"

Lumpy looked up from his ginger snap. "The shed I suspect, probably as flammable as...Jesus."

The cushion exploded inches from the shed; feathers blew up like a fountain of grey volcanic ash. Flames appeared from nowhere, licking the sides of the shed.

I stared across the garden to see Puss running for cover, whiskers singed and both the Bag Lady and Betty clutching cremated tofu kebabs in shock. And before I had a chance to grab anything let alone think of what to grab, Lumpy was outside clutching a pot of tea and the kettle.

Mavis, mid hair straightening, looked up as I raced into the room.

"What the hell was that?" she said as I charged out of the patio windows with a few bottles grabbed from the fridge.

"Grab the basin," I shouted to Mavis.

"What?"

"The basin – in the sink."

Lumpy emptied the kettle, then flung milk, tea, Coke, several dips, and whatever other liquid he could find onto the fire. Betty handed him the vodka in a panic – Lumpy glared and shouted, "The blanket."

The Bag Lady dragged an armful from the tent, coughing from the dust. Lumpy threw one after the other onto the fire, sending the last of the feathers singed and black into the air.

Puss peered from my bedroom window with a terrified look.

"I think that's caught it," Lumpy said with a final plop of the last blanket.

Mavis emptied the basin with a "just in case" sigh on top; the heap hissed. "You always were good with a blanket," she muttered.

Half her hair was straightened; the other half still curly fluttered in the wind. Lumpy smiled at her and she smiled back.

We stared at the charred remains as bubbling mint sauce and Coke oozed from beneath a blanket. It was inches from the shed, now completely black on one side. Smoke belched across it like a grey mist, while Puss still at the window was now mouthing a silent meow.

"Must have been the methylated spirits," said Betty.

"Methylated..." I said.

"Or the petrol," muttered the Bag Lady.

"Petrol?" I shouted.

"Yes, well we wanted a decent send-off – fire terms-like."

"Send-off. Another minute and the shed would have gone up."

"You hated that shed," said the Bag Lady, "you said that the flood had knocked the stuffing out of it."

"What do you mean stuffing?" I said.

"You said it was Rodger's shed and both he and it could get stuffed."

"That's not the same thing."

Mavis, now holding Lumpy's hand again, laughed, stating that burnt wood was all the rage. "They are always doing it on *Grand Designs*," she said, "and it's waterproof."

"Still, if it wasn't there – there would be room for something better," said the Bag Lady.

"Like a hot tub," said Betty.

The Bag Lady gave her a "shut it" nudge.

Puss didn't venture out for days after the fire; even pakoras wouldn't entice her. Instead she stared at the window and cowered whenever she saw the Bag Lady strike a match.

I banned the frypan and all outside cooking apart from heating water for tea.

"Gone are the days of fry-ups and sausages," I said to her and Betty. "I'll shout you when tea is ready, and you can like it or lump it."

Betty looked downcast.

The Bag Lady huffed. "You can't fry fish the way I do," she said, "and what will Puss eat – from a tin?"

"Well it is what most cats do," I said.

Mavis said nothing. She was in the lounge room with Lumpy – getting her things together.

Chapter Twenty-One

THE CONTROL FREAK

A mother's pride is often a daughter's curse.

The Bag Lady, Betty, and I were munching on the last of our "anything without coconut" takeaway. They were both eating with their hands, which apparently was now all the rage, while I was eating a crispy lentil Bhaji minus mint sauce.

We sat close to the fire, waiting to feel the warmth.

The fire was now in a coal scuttle and enclosed by a set of bricks, and the heat, it seemed, stopped at the bricks. The Bag Lady was huddled over the fire covered in jackets (to make a point), while Betty (also making a point) was making shivering noises.

I watched the Bag Lady slip the last portion into her mouth. I (to prove my point) threw off my jacket, stuck a fork in my bhaji, and took a bite.

Hmm...

The Bag Lady poked at the fire with disdain. She was giving me the silent treatment.

That morning, as I was heading for the bin to dispose of last night's pasanda (a coconut affair of poor quality), I looked across the garden and instead of seeing the Bag Lady and Betty drinking tea, I saw a black shed, a zipped-up tent, and last night's bonfire still smouldering.

I decided enough was enough and spent the morning standing

outside the tent with a large bin bag as the Bag Lady dumped her frypan and pots in it. She hadn't spoken to me since.

"How far have you come since the bookshop," I said, pretending to be warm. "The good old days singing in front of the shop in the rain – can't do that now," I said, "not with the new owner."

"I don't need to sing now," said the Bag Lady. "Betty and I have bigger fish to fry." She glared at me. "Well we did."

"You only have yourself to blame," I muttered.

The Bag Lady tightened her jacket around her, tossed her takeaway wrappers onto the fire, and huffed.

"That woman is an inspiration," she muttered.

I looked at Betty. "What would you know about inspiration?"

"Plenty," she said.

"Aye, plenty," muttered the Bag Lady.

I stared in disbelief; the only inspiration Betty was into was gossip. When not sitting by the fire talking about it, she spent her time dragging Bingo about the streets of Lochgilphead looking for it.

Bingo was Shifty's dog, who was the size of a terrier and at least ten years old. Jumping for him was a pipe dream, chewing a bone a long-distance memory, and walking was a painful affair. Betty didn't care; she walked the dog senseless – claiming that it was good for his arthritis. Truth was she was nosy and loved to scour the streets daily.

She had watched Amanda transform the bookshop from the beginning. Every day she trekked past the window and peered in and, if lucky, scrounged a water bowl for Bingo.

She had even, on a good day, when Amanda was not at the shop, managed to drag Bingo to Amanda's house. It was a little out of the way for Bingo's short legs, but with a couple of digestive biscuits Betty managed to persuade Bingo to "go the extra mile." Where not only did she scrounge a water bowl for Bingo but a coffee from "freshly ground beans of Amanda's own mix."

"She has done a great job," said Betty. She rattled the coal scuttle with a shiver. "You should see her place."

"I have, it's empty," I said.

"Aye, but that was in the dark."

"Still empty," I said.

Betty turned to the Bag Lady. "The garden's been transformed, that woman is a marvel."

"Absolute marvel," muttered the Bag Lady.

"She's got a goat now and some hens – and is going to sell free-range everything once the hubby is back. She even has an honesty box put up" – Betty threw me a look – "right by her bonfire site."

"Nobody has a bonfire site," I said.

"She burns stuff there all the time."

"That doesn't make it a site."

"She said I could come and burn anything I want – anytime. She says fires are organic."

"What else would they be," I said.

"And we should share the organic-ness of it all."

"What?"

"Yes, it's all in her chakras." Betty pointed her poppadum at me. "She is a fire person."

"A fire person," muttered the Bag Lady.

I sighed as Mavis and Lumpy appeared.

They had gone home – hand-holding – in search of blankets for the Bag Lady and came back with a boot full. Lumpy silently dumped the blankets at the tent and Mavis without a word went into the kitchen and came out with coffee for all.

Mavis's mother, Cat, had had a turn and it was *coach* she was asking for, not Mavis.

Lumpy reminded Cat of an old PE teacher who had mentored her through her sports "heyday." And now in the later stages of her dementia, she often thought Lumpy was him and would insist on doing the handshake of strength, which had Lumpy pulling faces of pain. According to Mavis, Cat had a grip like an arm wrestler – refusing to cut her nails didn't help.

I had heard so much about Mavis's mother that I felt I knew her. She had been a lover of sport, or as Mavis put it, anything that involved a racket, a short skirt, and teaming up with men. And it seemed that Mavis, a sports hater, was a great disappointment to her.

"My mother could never understand why I hated games, especially anything to do with a ball," said Mavis, handing around the coffee.

"Never trust a sporty person," said the Bag Lady.

"When I was ten she sent me to a tennis class – in a dress from a neighbour which was so tight I couldn't breathe let alone run. And they all fought over who had to partner with me."

"Can't picture you playing tennis," said Betty.

"One even smashed his racket against the wall." She smiled with discomfort. "Tossed a ball at me."

She handed around the biscuits.

"'I'd rather eat a dead pigeon than play with her,' he said."

"Such a rubbish game," said Betty.

"Sad thing was I agreed with them – who would want to play with me?"

"Yes, well we are not ten now are we," said Lumpy.

"I couldn't even catch a ball let alone hit one," said Mavis. "I stood there like a lump of invisible lard as they shouted and argued. In the end, I hid in the shed. It took three months of coming home covered in grease and ball stains before Mum would listen."

Lumpy sighed; he'd heard it all before.

"Sport people are so self-righteous," muttered the Bag Lady.

"Mum was always telling me to go off and play. Even now when I visit her, she tells me to find something to do so she can talk to "the coach.""

Mavis nudged the packet of biscuits at Lumpy.

"Your mum's just a man's woman, that's all," said Lumpy.

"So you say," said Mavis.

"Never trust a man's woman," said the Bag Lady.

Lumpy looked at his watch. Fanny had organised a family meeting. "Complications," muttered Lumpy. "Things aren't good."

"Of course, Fanny plays tennis like a pro," muttered Mavis. "She even taught the bloody game for a while – helped pay for her massage training."

Lumpy gave her a sad smile. "Yes, well we won't be talking about tennis today, will we?"

"Families," muttered the Bag Lady.

"Tell me about it," said Mavis.

Chapter Twenty-Two

THE FALL AND RISE OF A BOOKSHOP

Change is a bastard when not chosen.

The bookshop is the carbuncle I wanted to avoid and, like all carbuncles, avoiding it was impossible; in the end, it had to be faced, squeezed, followed by a good seeing-to.

Betty said I was "talking in riddles." The Bag Lady asked exactly what I thought a good seeing-to was, because in her book it "had nothing to do with squeezing plooks," while Sheryl looked up 'carbuncle' on the Internet. In the end, I stopped texting and arranged to go to the opening with Sheryl.

I could have gone with Betty and the Bag Lady, but as they were now on the opening committee – which consisted of two – I opted out.

The Bag Lady and Betty were right up Amanda's proverbial street. They had collected bucketloads of money. It seemed that everyone this side of Oban had a yearning for a hot tub, a free takeaway, and/or a makeover from Fyne Hands, where the local beautician claims not only that "beauty is just a rub away" but that a "tan can perk the un-perkable" and that a piercing, in the right place, "can bring life not only to one's belly but to one's sex life as well."

The Bag Lady and Betty had, to quote Amanda, "smashed the record into six figures" and she was "over the moon."

"Let's start the day with a bang," said Amanda, who then arranged to pick up the committee at "eight-ish" for *all-American* waffles for breakfast followed by balloon-blowing and hanging at the bookshop.

Not much happens in Lochgilphead, so a shop relaunching with as much publicity as Amanda had organised had everyone wanting to go – apart from Mavis and me.

Over several weeks, Amanda had placed a series of articles in the *Fyne News* building up to a full-page spread about the opening day.

Sheryl's Steven was excited; he had just published his third cosy mystery in the Wild West and Amanda had booked him for her first authors reading.

"Our first real writer," she said, "and he's local," which she followed with a travel expenses joke.

Amanda was born in Dunoon and met Dan, an American navy man stationed there. After they married they moved to America and lived there long enough for Amanda to talk like one. The couple had only returned to Scotland after Dan began to search his ancestors and discovered he had Scottish blood, as Amanda liked to say, "pulsing through his veins and nether regions."

Amanda had a joke for every occasion, especially about her absent husband.

The first time Amanda advertised she wrote a small piece about "filling the black hole in the Mid Argyll book market." She said she wanted to "revive real books" and was eager for book requests from "all you guys out there."

In the following weeks, she promised "books you can't put down, writers, open mics, poetry slams, and anything else you can think of. Real events with real coffee." She wrote because, as she said, "In this digital age, the world is crying out for the people being people and the spoken word."

Two days before the opening, her final advert was splashed across the *Fyne News* centre page with an explosion of promises...

"The Grand Opening of Lochgilphead's New Book Centre
An Event for ALL"
Free colouring-in books for ALL

Dunoon's favourite wizard reading *Harry Potter*
A real live Where's Wally

As if anyone cares where he is...

and
A storyteller who did it with a drum.

"There is so much," wrote Amanda, "I don't know if we'll get through it all in one day! But there is one thing for sure, if you buy a raffle ticket you won't go away empty-handed. There'll be a free discount voucher for all who purchased with more prizes than I have free doughnuts. And I like my doughnuts."

Sheryl and I met outside the bookshop on Saturday. Mavis, who claimed to be "in two minds," said she "might come later"; I wasn't holding my breath. I hadn't seen her since her visit with her mother.

Lumpy however had been in the takeaway ordering for one. Mavis, he said, was in denial. "Her mother's dying, and all Mavis talks about is the tennis and laxatives."

Amanda had invited the librarians, school staff, and anyone who was anyone in the community centre. And they along with Sheryl and myself stood in the street staring at a large red, white, and blue ribbon tied in a bow across the entrance. It was a chilly March morning and the wind had picked up, flapping the balloons outside. The pipe band could be heard in the distance. After a rousing marching song, they appeared around the corner with their kilts swinging. A police car followed with its siren silently turning along with Where's Wally and the Dunoon Wizard skipping about the car.

The song finished with an extra-long drum roll as the pipe band arrived at the shop.

The crowd clapped as the police car gently reversed, easing into a puddle.

The Dunoon Wizard opened the door to Charlie, a six-year-old in a wheelchair, and Madge, an eighty-year-old with a Zimmer frame. It took time for the two to clutter out, giving Where's Wally a chance to mime something Scottish with a couple of balloons. After which the primary head teacher made a speech about the joy of feeling paper "between one's fingers." Then, after several "what am I to do again" looks from Madge, the ribbon was cut with both her and Charlie clutching an extra-large pair of scissors – courtesy of Danny's Hardware Store.

The pipe band then after a series of more drum rolls struck up a a rousing version of "Stop Yer Tickling, Jock," which the wizard began to mime along to until Madge joined in.

It was an impressive beginning; enough, as the head teacher said, "to make one forget about the wind." And as the remains of the bow trailed into the puddles, we all followed inside.

Amanda stood behind her counter which had a large suggestion box with "Please Feed Me" plastered across it.

I was gutted.

The shop was so much bigger and better than I expected, and the coffee better than Betty has poured me. Amanda was winning everyone over in schoolgirl pigtails and fairy kirby grips; a hairstyle that, apart from her, no woman past thirty could get away with.

She laughed and joked with each person as they entered, offering them doughnuts filled with cream and jam – while eating one herself.

It was gut-wrenching; I mean, I have never seen anyone eat a doughnut and keep their lipstick on before. And there she was lipstick intact without one dribble or stray crumb.

"Welcome," she said with a warm American accent.

And before I had time to say thanks, cheers, or where did you get your kirby grips from, she was off like a pixie on speed, greeting each person by name.

"She's a poet," said Madge, peering over a vampire thriller, which had a cover of heaving breasts and a male six-pack. "And she knows every book in the shop."

"Well she is the owner," I said.

"And she's going to do homemade cake and coffee."

"Very Waterstones," I muttered.

I spied Tenzam at the travel books section; he was flipping through *The Real Bangladesh Story* while talking to Charlie about how poor the villagers were.

"They don't waste a thing, drink rice water," said Tenzam.

Charlie manoeuvred himself down the shop.

Amanda was talking to Sheryl about the book group and how excited she was that Steven was the first, while Charlie, who had escaped from Tenzam, was explaining to Madge about how a poetry slam had nothing to do with slamming doors and an open mic "didn't have any backup, apart from maybe a guitar."

Madge, not hearing a word, pulled another vampire book from the shelf and flashed the heaving six-pack cover at Charlie. "What about slamming this?" she said.

Charlie reversed back to Lumpy, who was now standing with Tenzam looking at a book on Indian recipes.

Then Madge made for Amanda. "Charlie said you have some poets who like slamming things – what about vampires?"

Amanda offered Madge a doughnut and was just about to offer Sheryl one when Mavis appeared at the door, looking grumpy.

Chapter Twenty-Three

THE RAFFLE

One person's junk is another person's raffle prize.

*L*umpy, mid chat, had captured Charlie a second time and was in full swing about how they make a barbecue in Bangladesh out of bedsprings. Charlie's imagination was almost caught.

Tenzam, by the doughnuts with Kamal, looked embarrassed. "It was not bedsprings, it was the back of the fridge," he said. "And it was just the once."

"And when they eat," continued Lumpy, "they use their hands. Of all the food you would eat with your hands, why choose rice? And yet I have never seen a cleaner plate than Tenzam's."

Charlie's attention waned.

"It's an incredible sight. They pressed the rice into a ball..."

Charlie began to reverse his chair.

"...apparently it tastes better that way," shouted Lumpy at his back.

"Yes, well I tried it and ended up with half of it on my jacket," muttered Mavis.

I asked her how her mother was – Lumpy pulled a "don't go there" face.

"Turns out the turn was more of a run," she said in a quiet voice. "Of course, Fanny saved the day with charcoal tablets."

Sheryl pulled a face...

"Then Mum started on about 'coach,'" said Mavis. "She told me to go out and play – while she'd sort things out with him. 'This is Lumpy, not the coach,' I told her, 'we're getting married.' Then Fanny dragged me out of the room and gave me an earful, telling me to be *dementia-friendly*. 'You should take a leaf out of Lumpy's book and *go with the flow*,' she said." Mavis looked at me. "'So Lumpy should go on having his hand crushed,' I said."

"It was not about hand-crushing." Lumpy sighed.

"She really gets my goat," said Mavis. "I mean what does she know."

"She is a therapist," said Sheryl."

"Just because she can massage a toe into submission doesn't mean she has an understanding of dementia."

Sheryl walked away.

"Doughnut?" said Tenzam to Lumpy.

"Fanny is right," said Lumpy.

"Typical – you always take her side."

"Mavis, there is no side."

"Doughnut?" Kamal gestured to Mavis.

"That is a brownie," said Tenzam. "This is a doughnut."

Mavis made a snappy comment about sugar being twice as nice as spice.

Kamal laughed.

"Typical," muttered Lumpy.

Mavis glared at him.

Neither said a word.

Amanda picked up the plate. "Can I offer either of you...something?"

Lumpy didn't notice.

Mavis waved her away with her hand.

"I'll have one," said Charlie, reversing past.

Mavis pulled the book Lumpy was holding from him. "*A Spice for Every Occasion*." She looked at him. "How can I compete?"

Lumpy eyed Kamal. "How can I?"

"Typical." Mavis huffed. "You have an answer for everything."

"So do you."

The bookshop fell silent; people began to look.

"Time for the raffle," shouted Amanda, "anyone want to pull the first ticket? Charlie, Madge?"

"I am not even in the running with you anymore – am I?" muttered Mavis.

"I didn't even think it was a race," said Lumpy with a hushed voice.

Mavis snapped the book closed and nodded towards me. "Neff says I can stay there for a while."

Lumpy looked at me with sad eyes.

I was about to ask Mavis when did I say that, when Lumpy took the book from Mavis and walked to the counter to buy it.

"Perhaps you should go then," he muttered.

"Perhaps I will," she muttered.

We didn't stay after that; Mavis pretty much bullied me into leaving, not that I was bothered. The last place I wanted to be was standing in the "book centre" watching Mavis have a meltdown in the middle of a raffle draw.

I mean I didn't even have a ticket.

Kamal followed us out in disgust. "I bought ten raffles tickets," he said, "and nothing, not a thing but a voucher for a book. What sort of raffle is that?"

Mavis lingered at the car for a moment. "A book is better than nothing," she muttered.

Kamal handed her the voucher. "Maybe you can use it then."

I stared at the man, slick and polished, as he opened the car door for Mavis and watched her climb in.

I wondered what he was after – Kamal was always after something.

Chapter Twenty-Four

THE SPICE RACK: PART TWO

A spice rack in Bangladesh is unheard of.

I arrived home from work that night to the sort of conversation any sane person would run a mile from. The Bag Lady and Betty had spent the night with Mavis in my kitchen. I dumped the carry-out on the table, pulled a bottle of wine out, and waved it at the girls.

They looked up with a "thank God you're here and with wine" sigh.

Mavis didn't even notice I had arrived. She had been at the sherry, and although the Bag Lady had offered coffee, tea, and toast, Mavis had refused all – draining my sherry supply was all she was interested in.

"He said, 'what about the spice rack? Who was I thinking of when I made that, the postman?' 'Didn't we make it,' I said, then he made an 'if you call watching helping' joke, so I stupidly told him he could take the spice rack and shove it."

Mavis started to cry...

"I think I went too far, but I had to carry on – didn't I?"

Mavis slumped into her chair.

The Bag Lady pushed Puss off her knee with a "now's my chance to leave" look.

Mavis and Lumpy had words as she went around to pick up some things. And it all started, it seemed, with a spice rack.

"I threw all the spices in the bin. 'This is for herbs,' I shouted. He shouted back, 'It's a spice rack...the clue is in the name.' Then he told me I can shove it!"

Mavis turned to the Bag Lady.

"Don't know what I would have done without you. You've listened to me all this time, not a word." She put her hand on the Bag Lady's; a tear fell onto the back of the Bag Lady's hand. "You're so kind."

"What about me?" said Betty.

"And me?" I said. "You've just drunk all my sherry."

"You hate sherry," said the Bag Lady, pulling Puss back onto her knee.

"He'll never forgive me, not after the spice rack."

"Spice rack?" said Betty.

"The one we made...when we first started" – she wiped her eyes – "cooking together." Mavis let out a deep sigh. "Back in the days of rosemary and bay leaves." She sniffed.

"Wine?" I said, pushing the carry-out into the middle of the table. "Madras, naan?"

Mavis wiped her eyes. "I'll stick with the crisps," she muttered.

I poured her a small glass. I poured myself, the Bag Lady, and Betty a large glass. The Bag Lady began to stroke Puss into cat heaven.

"Lumpy never shouts."

The Bag Lady pushed the crisp bag towards Mavis, then dipped her crisp into the madras and allowed Puss to lick it.

Mavis blew hard into her tissue.

"It will blow over," I said.

"He loved that spice rack, now suddenly it's trash, to be tossed aside...like me."

Mavis pulled the spice rack from her bag and everything else from her bag cascaded to floor. "So I took it with me..."

The Bag Lady picked up a photo of Lumpy and placed it on Mavis's knee as I filled her glass to the top.

"I made a nice rack once – at woodwork – the teacher was nuts," said Betty.

"I told him it was all over," said Mavis. "And he said he was glad. How could he be glad?"

"He was a funny man," Betty continued. "Who loved to make women laugh. 'Who needs looks,' he used to say, 'when you can make people wet themselves?'"

Even Mavis looked at her.

"Which was just as well," said Betty. "He was no oil painting – legs like a chicken. He was in the local panto too. He was most famous for his Dick Whittington. His 'Dick was to die for,' he used to say, then fall about laughing."

"And that was the calibre of his jokes?" sniffed the Bag Lady.

The Bag Lady's earthy humour came and went, like the weather. The first time I told her the Deep Heat joke she laughed so much she had to retreat to her teepee for fear of wetting herself. The second time she retreated in disgust.

"He died on stage," said Betty, "in the tennis scene."

The Bag Lady nudged her. "Don't mention tennis."

" – everyone saw it coming. He skidded and ended up head first in the net, it twisted around his neck..." Betty jumped up, acting out a strangulation scene. "...like this."

Puss jolted – the Bag Lady chuckled, coaxing Puss back to sleep.

"His racket flew into the rafters..."

"Don't mention the word 'racket' either."

"...knocked the lights out...a bulb hit one of the cast and shattered into...." She paused, looking at Mavis's sad face. "...all sorts of things."

Mavis gave her a weak smile.

"The cast never got over it. A plague was erected at the front of the school stage."

"Don't you mean plaque," I said.

"A man with a stance for the funny, if only we saw it," Betty muttered.

The Bag Lady coughed.

"It's all true."

The Bag Lady coughed again. "Men," she muttered.

"Tell me about it," said Mavis and burst into tears.

The spice rack remained in the lounge when Mavis went to bed; it sat in the log bin, poised for the next fire. Mavis insisted that it remain there. And the next morning, as I lit the fire, I wondered if I should hide it.

Chapter Twenty-Five

THE COUCH

The time to worry about sanity is when you start to enjoy daytime TV.

A week later Mavis had taken up residence on my couch, which had by then moulded to her body. Every night I arrived home to find Mavis sprawled out like a Greek goddess with Puss at her feet. Mavis was retreating into herself and Puss was making the most of it.

I had two women to feed, little money, and a cat with the taste buds of millionaire. Puss sniffed at nothing but the best. And now that the Bag Lady's barbecued chicken wings were no longer on the menu she had taken to standing by her dish of tinned whatever and glaring at me.

While Mavis, "staying sober," was drowning her sorrows in my herbal tea collection.

Lumpy and Mavis had spent the week going around in circles texting each other: Mavis telling Lumpy how wrong he was and how right she was, followed by a lot of pining, and Lumpy telling her how much better things were now he didn't have to listen to her telling him how wrong he was.

"I just delete your messages," he texted. Which resulted in a flying mobile, Puss running for cover, and Mavis descending into a dark mood I had never seen before.

She wanted Lumpy to show his love by giving her what she wanted, while he wanted her to stop nagging. Finally, after the "delete your messages" text, she gave up texting. Instead she spent the whole day staring at the TV which wasn't always on. I had refused to pay for anything other than a TV license and she was fed up with seventies reruns on Freeview. She would sit in protest and then stare at her phone, hoping for a message, until she remembered the "switch you off" text.

Lumpy spent his time wandering into the takeaway hoping to bump into Mavis, which was highly unlikely, as she totally hated curries and the last person she wanted to see was Tenzam.

Mavis, it seems, was the only person in the universe who didn't like him. She blamed him as much as Lumpy for the split, claiming that "all men are bastards," which was during her "what alcohol have you got in the house" phase.

In one week, Mavis had been through many phases, including the heartbroken phase, the "loss of a dream" phase, and the "I don't want to go out of the house" phase, which was still "ongoing." All were best completed in private, unless you had a friend like me – a friend still fresh enough from a breakup to be forgiving, tolerant, and deaf.

Ignoring my "hi," Mavis moved in a comatose fashion from the couch to the kitchen, her only exercise for the day. She drank gallons of black tea, in the same mug, hardly bothering to wash it out. And the mug was as black as the Bag Lady's fingernail.

"My sister reckons alcohol causes eye-bags, and at my present state I need to protect the goods." I looked at Mavis, who was also touching on the "completely unrealistic" phase. She hadn't even put on a bra in three days, and for a woman of her vintage, "the goods" needed a little help.

"She says all marriages are about fights," said Mavis with a robust jiggle of her teabag. "What would she know – our first fight led to this." She tossed her teabag across the room; it slapped on the wall and then landed with a plop by the bin.

I took a few tolerant breaths.

"Pebble-dashing my kitchen?"

"You always make your jokes so flippant," she said with a stab at the honey jar. She dribbled the spoon from the jar to her mug, oblivious to the trail.

"Everything is about her – being right," she said, scuffing her way back to the couch. Puss shifted as she slid her legs across the couch and then made herself at home on her stomach.

Mavis took a loud slurp at her tea, a habit she'd recently acquired, while staring at the Freeview, then stroked Puss, who purred in pleasure.

"Being married is proving you're right even when you're not – isn't that what she said, Puss?" (Mavis was also in the "mad talking to things that don't answer back" phase.)

I sighed, turned the TV on, threw her the remote, and fell into the most uncomfortable and only available seat left in the room – with great tolerance.

"She says arguing is good for a marriage, like she can talk. Look at her marriage."

I told Mavis to stop talking about her sister as I was fed up hearing about a woman I hadn't met and thanks to her didn't want to. A woman who according to Mavis was married to a yes-man until he finally found a yes-woman, and they apparently, after not one argument, hooked up and are still together.

"So much for her theory," said Mavis. "Miss know-it-all."

I asked Mavis how old she was. She didn't answer but called me flippant again and then asked if I could take my Jaipuri outside, it was making her feel sick.

I stood by the opened patio doors and stared at the Bag Lady. She gave me a wave by her fire. Having her in my home had taken some getting used to. Maybe it was the same with Mavis.

"I told her we were postponing things," Mavis said. "On account of Mum-like."

Puss meowed and then looked at me with an "are you going to eat all of that?" look. Mavis, with an absent-minded pat, sculled her tea and then looked at her empty mug.

I wondered if my kitchen wall could take another used teabag.

"Your sister – is she as house-proud as you?" I asked.

"She's so house-proud she has no visitors. She always visits and takes ages to leave."

"Maybe you're more alike than you think."

With a dramatic cough, she looked at me. "That's the cruellest thing you have ever said. She has no sympathy and no understanding. She thinks this" – Mavis gestured with her thankfully empty mug – "is just a tiff."

"You did call it a break."

Mavis sighed and began to flick through the channels, stopping at *Murder She Wrote*.

"Mum's asking for him. Apparently there are things she can only tell the coach."

Chapter Twenty-Six

THE CURSE OF THE SHERRY BOTTLE

Good looks are wasted on the blind.

About a month after the split, Lumpy marched into the takeaway and handed me a bag of Mavis's belly dancing things. With a resigned look, he dumped the bag on the counter. Tenzam and I silently watched as a coin belt clattered to the floor. Lumpy with a sigh picked it up, thrusted it back into the bag, and left.

It was a turning point that sent Mavis into attacking what was left of my "unwanted raffle prize" sherry collection – *the real reason I never buy raffle tickets*. Without a word, she took the bag and my sherry into her room and didn't come out for the rest of the night.

For the next week, Lumpy continued to bring in more of Mavis's things. Each night as I arrived home with another bag, Mavis's face fell. And with an "I'll pay you back once I can face the world again" mutter, Mavis would retreat into my spare room.

Mavis had given up, closed down like a redundant post office. And it was not something I was used to. I mean, Mavis worked in the post office; she was born to chat, gossip, and laugh. She loved people and their business. Now she had no interest in anything except how many bottles of sherry were left. She had even let one the Zumba pupils take all her shifts at the post office.

Lumpy embraced the split by throwing personal care to the wind. He stopped shaving, wore sandals, and spent his time flicking the mop about the community centre like a wet sock, claiming that "he was having a ball."

Finally, on Sunday night, after a week of purging himself of all things "Mavis," he appeared in overalls that looked like they had been scrunched up in a ball and tossed over a hedge for a hoofed animal to trample on. He was like an apparition from Woodstock.

"How will she come back if you get about like a scarecrow?" I said.

He pushed a bag of CDs onto the counter with a "just give it to her" look.

"Why don't you?" I said, pushing the bag back to him. "You should be talking to her," I said, checking out her choice of belly dancing music. "And besides, you have the CD player."

Lumpy didn't answer, instead with a face as long as Tenzam's spice order demanded a naga, "the hotter the better," as he wanted to "celebrate" with a "curry that would burn the pipes."

"Celebrate?" I said. "Why?"

Lumpy sighed. "Singledom."

"That's nothing to celebrate."

"You think," said Lumpy.

"A few months down the line you'll be kicking yourself," I said.

"As if."

"There is only so much fun you can have with a TV remote to yourself," I lied. (I'd give anything to have mine back.)

Lumpy looked unconvinced.

"You look miserable – just like Mavis."

"Aye, that you do," nodded the Roadworks Man.

"As if," Lumpy snorted. "Being single is a total blast."

I stared at his unkempt beard and wondered who he was trying to convince. He looked thin, in a "can't be bothered to eat" way, and I wondered how much of his hotter-than-bonfire curry he would actually eat.

Not that Mavis was much better – she had nosedived into a place that scared me. She'd stopped plucking her eyebrows and let her face go all hairy above the lip. She even let her hair colour grow out.

Who was worse I had no idea.

"She calls the spare room her room now," I said.

"Who cares," said Lumpy.

"And she doesn't eat, she calls my cheese sauce custard and my vegetables mush."

"So?" sniffed Lumpy and headed to his car for more "belly dancing riff-raff."

"She's not coping," I shouted at him. "She's even been to the doctor for pills and more time off work."

The door slammed behind him.

I stared at the door and made a mental note to go to the co-op. The buy-one-get-one-free sherry sale was on its last day.

As Lumpy headed out to the car for more bags, Kamal appeared. He took one look and mumbled something in Bengali.

Kamal spent most of his time in Ban Duic sitting at the corner table shouting into his mobile – except on Sundays.

We opened late on Sundays. Tenzam was always there before me, stirring a bubbling pot with his ear pressed to his mobile and shouting in Bengali. And on a Sunday it was Kamal at the other end of the phone.

"He's coming," he'd shout like it was a hurricane. "Can you bag up the money?"

Then we would spend the rest of the shift anxiously looking at the door and jumping when it opened. Who knew when Kamal would appear, angry, annoyed, and ready to moan about the takings.

Kamal was a moody man whose handsome face could just as easily snarl as smile. He had a way of flicking through the takings that oozed annoyance, and I learnt to avoid him as much as possible.

Of course, tripping over Mavis's bags didn't help.

"How do I work with all this here?" he said, crashing the till open.

He nudged the bags on the desk and they tumbled to the ground – scarves and coin belts spilled out onto the floor.

"This is a takeaway, not a harem," he said and then mumbled something about health and safety.

The Roadworks Man threw me a look.

Lumpy entered stony-faced; he silently dumped another bag onto the counter, let out a long sigh, and began to collect what was on the floor.

Kamal looked up from the till, saw Lumpy and a smile flickered across his face.

"Women," he said.

According to Tenzam, Kamal had been through a few.

"They are unpredictable, like spices," said Kamal. "Why do you think we keep them out of the restaurant?"

The Roadworks Man muttered something about me and my "woman's touch" which went over everyone's head, except of course mine.

Kamal continued on about how "making a woman happy" was "the impossible dream, a mountain with no end" and that "in the end only a mother was worth the effort."

"Making a woman happy is like cooking," said Kamal. "Too much heat and you burn the flavour."

Which I thought was ironic since I had never seen him lift a kettle, let alone a frypan. And as for making a woman happy? Kamal's smile lasted minutes – if you were lucky. In fact, the only time I had ever seen him really happy was when the rugby team had ordered a takeaway and told him to keep the change. Even the Deep Heat joke, which seemed to impress every man who entered the takeaway, left him unmoved. His good looks were a complete waste of genes; once he opened his mouth, you just wanted him to go away.

"Aye that's right, don't let the bastards grind you down," said the Roadworks Man with a glance at Kamal.

"Bastards?" said Lumpy.

"Well yes, I mean once a woman starts on your day, well...err...your day is no longer your own – is it?"

Which I thought was rich coming from a man who slept on his

own, and from what I could see, not by choice. The Roadworks Man practically lived at the takeaway. His home was a bedsit above the restaurant linked up to the restaurant's Wi-Fi. He even started putting the restaurant bins out like the restaurant was his home. He was so lonely he cornered the postman on Saturday for coffee.

In fact, apart from Tenzam's ability to milk his loveable appeal – and double his income in tips – the others had as much luck with women as I had with a job.

Lumpy was half the man he used to be. And Kamal spent most of his time shouting in his mobile too – usually about money. He was always angry, and I got the distinct impression women were the reason.

I told them that their understanding of woman had got them were they were today and was about to tell them where that was when they, in unison said, "Exactly" – missing the point completely.

I gave up.

The phone rang; I handed it to the owner.

"It's for you," I said. "He said if you don't pay him today he is going to come – rip your chillies from the fridge and shove them one at a time in a very uncomfortable place."

None of which Kamal understood; however, as it was a he and not a she, Kamal, with a blank face, switched off the phone and tossed it across the bench.

I told Mavis about Kamal and his mountains. I tried to make her laugh, elaborated about the phone call and the Roadworks Man.

"Kamal is a man in his own right," she muttered. "There are not many like him."

Chapter Twenty-Seven

THE SPICE RACK: PART 3

Time is a great healer, but only for those who have the time.

That night we sat outside by the fire, putting off going in. None of us wanted to go and leave Mavis looking sad and miserable.

"Time is a great healer," muttered the Bag Lady.

"And perhaps," said Betty, "the universe is telling you something."

The Bag Lady threw her a look. They'd had numerous arguments about the universe and why "we" (humans in general) were here. Betty, at present, went with a "we are all here for a purpose" theory while the Bag Lady had taken up a more "who knows, who cares" philosophy. They both swithered between the two – which is what happens when you spend all your time sitting by a fire staring at the stars.

Mavis had been to see her mother, a first since the split. I drove her and brought her back along with a fish supper. Meeting Mavis's mother for the first time had been an experience.

I had heard so much about her – mostly that she had little time left and was a dragon. And there she was, sitting up in bed like she had decades to live, smiling like she had just heard the Deep Heat joke and approved.

She had a round face like Mavis, except now the skin was stretched across it. The same hair as Mavis except it was white, and hard sharp eyes – nothing like Mavis's.

She was surrounded by photos, most of herself, apart from one of Mavis in her belly dancing dress; it was hidden behind a picture of Fanny and her children.

I was surprised...

"Lumpy gave it to her," said Mavis. "She's always hiding it; the nurses have found it in all sorts of places, behind the toilet being the favourite."

I put it back behind the "Fanny photo" as Cat asked yet again for the "Coach." She had spent the whole afternoon asking for him, along with telling us how Fanny "sorted things." Finally, Mavis, tearful and broken, left. I was about to follow when Cat grabbed my arm and pointed to the photo of Mavis.

"Tell her to bring back her scarves next time," muttered Cat, "no one twirls a scarf like my Mavis."

Mavis tossed her chip into the fire and watched it sizzle.

"I told Fanny to cancel the cake, and the Taj Mahal. She said Lumpy had already told her – 'the expert,' as he likes to call her." She wiped her mouth. "No wonder I am finished with him, that man is about as much support as a Primark bra."

Mavis screwed up her fish supper wrapper and tossed it in the fire. She then went into the house and came out with the spice rack.

She stood in front of the fire now sizzling with chips wrappings.

"He used to make me coffee the way I like it. We used to laugh, and dance. He said my scarf twirling memorised him."

She waved the spice rack about the air. "Not anymore. If he doesn't care, so neither do I – it's over."

She made to toss the rack into the fire.

The Bag Lady grabbed her arm. "Don't."

"Wait," said Betty. "You said he was a man of unfathomable depths."

"I was drunk."

"Swept you off his feet," said the Bag Lady.

"What about his cheese sauce?" I said. I was clutching at straws.

"He doesn't even look at cheese anymore."

"Maybe it's a phase," I said, still clutching at straws.

"He has stopped listening." She turned the spice rack over in her hand. "I thought he cared, now I don't care that he doesn't."

I remembered how happy they were. How he loitered around the belly-dance classes with his overalls clean and ironed looking for her. How he used to come into the class with the excuse of bleeding the radiators just to watch her dance.

I took the spice rack from her. "Let me use it," I said. "It's so pretty."

Mavis pulled it from me, paused, and then tossed it onto the fire. "That's that," she said to herself.

We stared at the spice rack as the paint began to peel from the heat.

"One good thing," muttered Mavis. "I don't have to put up with my sister and her take-the-piss cake."

I wanted to say something but couldn't think of anything.

Instead we stared at the fire as the flames licked around the sides of the rack until it collapsed.

Puss's purring filled the silence...

"You can always get a new one," muttered the Bag Lady.

"Or give up spice altogether," said Mavis.

Chapter Twenty-Eight

THE ROD MAN

The silent treatment never works for men, they just embrace it.

The next day I was standing in an empty Taj Mahal. It was a Monday night with only the Roadworks Man parked at his usual table, along with Tenzam.

Tenzam was telling a story about his sister's wedding in Bangladesh, which neither the Roadworks Man or I was listening to, when Lumpy walked in with a weak smile.

I handed Lumpy a Coke and for the first time since the split, Lumpy didn't mention Mavis. Instead, he took a seat beside the Roadworks Man and glumly stared at a menu.

Tenzam pulled out his mobile and began to flick through pictures of a Bangladesh wedding feast. Biryanis, roasted goat's meat, and, according to Tenzam, the "largest, tastiest prawns" in the world.

Lumpy, still staring at the menu, ordered a mixed grill. Tenzam nodded and went back into the kitchen while I, making a point, looked for a pen.

Tenzam, as usual, had nicked it.

"These prawns," said the Roadworks Man, gesturing with his knife, "are the size of a dinner plate."

"Size is not everything," muttered Lumpy.

"With prawns it is," said the Roadworks Man, "isn't it Tenzam?" he shouted.

I answered the phone, moaning about the lack of pens. Tenzam pretended not to hear.

"Aye they're tasty alright," said the Roadworks Man. "Those villagers, they eat prawns by the bucketloads. That's what the cousin says. He used to travel."

I went into the kitchen and with a glare to match Tenzam's grabbed the only pen in the restaurant.

"They may have no money," the Roadworks Man said, "but they're rich" – he patted his chest – "in here."

"I can see that," said Lumpy with a flat voice.

I entered with a sizzling plate held above my head. Smoke filled the restaurant as I edged myself between the fridge and the Roadworks Man's long legs – he didn't move an inch.

"You know the cousin?" said the Roadworks Man.

Lumpy shook his head.

"Aye you do – he sorted drains at the community centre during the great sewage flood."

I placed Lumpy's smoking plate in front of him.

"He's handy with a rod – some call him the Rod Man." The Roadworks Man pointed his fork at Lumpy. "He's been to India, hasn't he Tenzam?" he shouted.

The smoke alarm started; I began the standard tea-towel flapping under the alarm.

"India?" said Lumpy. "I thought you were talking about Bangladesh."

I continued to flap.

"Same thing, isn't it?" said the Roadworks Man.

I opened the front door and went back to my flapping.

Tenzam, using a broom handle – which stood behind the kitchen door for such purpose – knocked the smoke alarm. It whined into silence. Tenzam placed the broom in the most awkward position possible and looked at the Roadworks Man.

"No," said Tenzam, "they are different."

The Roadworks Man looked at Lumpy. "Sure, you remember the

drain man. Nothing stays blocked when he's about. He unblocked your missus' drains – don't you remember?"

"She's not my missus anymore," said Lumpy. He stared at Tenzam's mobile. "She wanted to go to the Shetlands for a honeymoon."

"Cosy," muttered the Roadworks Man, manipulating his naan across his plate.

"I'd much rather travel somewhere hot," said Lumpy.

"Aye well, it's not all it's cracked up to be," muttered the Roadworks Man. "The cousin ended up with a dodgy tummy."

"I always wanted to travel," said Lumpy.

"He had to come home early," said the Roadworks Man.

"I mean there is a lot to be said for the Asian culture," said Lumpy.

"Folk say that when they have never been," said the Roadworks Man.

"I mean what culture do we have here? Christmas? *X Factor*?"

Tenzam began to flick through the channels. He stopped at a Bollywood channel. A young Indian actress was dancing on a rooftop. She was wearing silk pyjamas which clung to her taut body thanks to a wind machine working overtime.

The Roadworks Man and Tenzam watched – without a word.

Lumpy, now flicking through Tenzam's photos, didn't look up.

"Nobody should look that good in pyjamas," I said.

No one heard.

"I mean look at these people," Lumpy said, gesturing to the phone, "real people doing real things with mud and stuff."

"Probably do their own unblocking, with reeds and bits of wood," muttered the Roadworks Man, his eyes still glued to the TV.

An older clip flashed onto the screen. Shah Rukh Khan and Kajol dancing in the rain. A famous couple who have danced in more Bollywood movies than Lumpy's had curries. They danced at a time when romance was more important than flesh. I watched Shah Rukh Khan kiss Kajol's neck, their clothes drenched enough to see his nipples. I had seen that dance many times, and Shah Rukh Khan's nipple always mesmerised me. That and his ability to kiss a neck like no other.

"Those are just photos from Facebook," said Tenzam.

"But they are real people," said Lumpy. "Visiting them would be way better than Shetland in a camper van. That woman has no sense of adventure."

"I wouldn't say that," said the Roadworks Man. "Mind the rugby club."

"I've never been overseas – haven't even been past Glasgow, except once to Cardiff for a rugby match," said Lumpy.

The dance clip changed to another Shah Rukh Khan and Kajol dance. They are older, moving through scenery reachable only by a plane, and there is not a nipple in sight. I began to wonder when the rain would start when Tenzam flicked the channel and a younger couple splashed on the screen. A girl in the shortest skirt ever.

"You should give Mavis one more try," I said.

"Trying is what that woman is," muttered Lumpy to himself.

I gave up; Lumpy was as interested in his broken-hearted ex as I was in the drain man's ability to unblock a drain. I decided to ignore the men and stopped talking to them altogether.

They didn't notice.

Lumpy, oblivious to all, talked about his plans to trek to Bangladesh and beyond without Miss "No Compromise" Mavis, while Tenzam was casually flicking through the channels, stopping at any dancing woman with little on.

"Bet you her drains don't get blocked," said the Roadworks Man, gesturing to the TV.

Tenzam laughed as the door burst open, allowing the rain to lash in. Amanda appeared windswept and laughing as her husband followed.

"We deserve a takeaway, don't we darling," she said.

The husband picked a menu.

Amanda looked at the TV.

We're back to the young woman on a rooftop again.

"Nobody should look that good in the rain," she said.

The Roadworks Man gestured to me. "That's what Herself says."

"Men," laughed Amanda. She looked at me, then touched her husband's arm.

The husband stared ahead.

Tenzam handed Amanda her carry-out with a sweet smile. She had ordered chapattis along with her usual "veggie dish" with no onions, salt, nuts, or ghee and boiled rice: "a Tenzam special," as she liked to call it.

Amanda peered into her takeaway bag, counted the chapattis, and smiled sweetly, "I have an aversion to fat," she said.

"All that ghee will block up your drains," chipped in the Roadworks Man.

All three men laughed as the Roadworks Man basked in his manly joke moment.

"My pipes don't need sorting," said Amanda, "they are fine as they are." She looked at her husband. "Aren't they, darling?"

The husband, still staring ahead, grunted.

"I hear you have a winner for the hot tub?" said the Roadworks Man.

Tenzam and Amanda flashed a "shut it" look.

"Yes; it'll be on our Facebook page tomorrow, and the *Fyne News*."

She flashed a look at Tenzam. "Betty has it all sorted."

The husband motioned her to go. "Come on," he said, "the football is starting."

"Betty?" I said.

"Yes, Betty has it all under control," muttered the husband, pressing a few notes into Tenzam's hand.

I watched the door slam behind them.

"I never imagined Betty sorting anything apart from laying out a packet of crisps for all to share," I said.

And for the first time in ages, Lumpy laughed.

Chapter Twenty-Nine

THE DIGGER

A machine in the hands of an idiot is like an instruction manual in a foreign language.

A few days later, I arrived home to find a mess at the back of my garden and a very clear understanding of what Amanda meant by "Betty had it sorted" – and it had nothing to do with crisps.

Betty and the Bag Lady had won the hot tub, and everyone knew apart from me. Even Tenzam was in on the surprise and had organised for me to spend the day in Oban with a huge shopping list while it was installed.

The Bag Lady and Betty wanted to cheer Mavis up and thought I would object, seeing as I moaned so much about the cost of things. Their plan was to surprise me with a hot tub lit up like a Christmas tree and firing on all cylinders.

Instead I walked into the garden to find a mound of dirt befitting the burial of a cat, with Betty, Mavis, and the Bag Lady glumly staring at it, Mavis with a look I had only seen once when she was dealing with a customer in the post office. A man who had been in the Argyll all afternoon and was convinced that he had already paid his road tax.

The Bag Lady and Betty had no idea that when a builder said, "no problem," it was the last thing he meant. And they had no idea about Mavis and her "I told you so" rants, which went on longer than the queen's speech.

"Builder's lingo," muttered Mavis. "It's a Labyrinth. Take time – it means nothing to them, a loose term that could mean anything within the next decade."

"He *was* recommended," said Betty. "How were we to know it was some has-been joiner who was two steps short of a Zimmer."

"His number came with the hot tub," said Mavis. "That's no recommendation, that's just a postman's note – probably getting a job for his mate."

According to Betty, the "so-called joiner" took a century to get out of the car, then after a mere glance at the garden said a digger was required to "straighten things out."

"A digger for an inflatable hot tub?" said Mavis.

The joiner, also deaf, ignored any protests, spent an hour saying "What you saying?" on his phone, mumbled something about "later," and left.

"Three hours later he returned," said the Bag Lady, "blocked the drive with a digger, drank a ridiculous amount of tea, and dug that."

The Bag Lady gestured to a flat space dug out from the bank at the back of the yard.

Mavis poked the dirt pile with her foot.

"Then," continued Betty, "he stumbled off the digger like he was having an asthma attack, answered his phone, and shouted, 'What you saying? A blowout?'"

"A digger," repeated Mavis, "for an inflatable hot tub?"

Betty threw Mavis a dirty look.

"Apparently blowouts are emergencies," said the Bag Lady.

"It's an inflatable, not the Sistine Chapel," said Mavis.

"He said he'd be back later," muttered the Bag Lady.

"Later to a builder is any time that is not today," said Mavis.

"Thanks for pointing that out," said Betty.

"Yes, a big help," muttered the Bag Lady.

We stared at the mound of dirt.

"Even a mole would be ashamed of that," said Mavis.

The two women glared at her.

"Never trust a builder," said Mavis. "They make rubbish brothers-in-law. That man never lifted a finger in my home, doors hung off the hinges, the toilet was so lopsided you needed a Zimmer to sit in it."

Mavis turned to me. "I had a leaking roof – for years – but would he help? Always an excuse; had to rely on the Roadworks Man, in the end."

"We thought the later meant later today," muttered the Bag Lady.

Mavis gave the pile dirt another poke; some crumbled down the side. "They're all the same. Full of it."

No one listened.

"Cowboys."

"He said the garden was complicated," continued Betty.

"Yes, well complicated means it will cost twice as much," said Mavis.

"Wonder what a blowout is?" muttered the Bag Lady.

Puss wandered past, dug into the pile of dirt, used it, and then sauntered off with barely a scratch to cover her mess.

"My sister said her ex was a fabulous builder," said Mavis. "Best in the business. Even when he left he still saw to her gutters."

The Bag Lady and Betty glared at her.

"I am fed up hearing about your sister," said the Bag Lady. "There'll be no talk of her in the hot tub."

"That space wouldn't even fit a footbath," Mavis said.

"And let me guess, your sister's got one," said Betty.

"She has two," said Mavis. "For her foot and head clients."

"Oh for Christ's sake, who hasn't got a footbath," snapped Betty and slung the last of her tea at Mavis's feet.

After Betty left, Mavis followed me into the kitchen and insisted on making me tea. She was fired up. I watched her stir my tea, then squeeze the bag within an inch of bursting.

"Builders, who needs 'em," she said, tossing the flattened teabag across the kitchen – it landed in the bin without touching the sides.

Mavis was angry, and for the first in ages it wasn't about her. She handed me my tea, then flattened the empty tea packet while talking about "her mission," because, as she said, "all builders are bastards."

I watched as Mavis's round frame seemed to energise with each sentence.

"I mean waiting is not an option" – she gestured to the Bag Lady – "not at their age; it's not like they're here forever, is it?"

She stopped and stared into the garden.

"I mean how long do you think Betty is going to be able to climb into a tub?"

"I thought the tub was for you," I said.

"And the Bag Lady – it's not like she's gonna see seventy again, is it? They could be dead before that geriatric installs the tub, and they have as much right to simmer under the stars as anyone."

She began to press the packet into a ball.

"Why should he stop them living their dream?"

"Their dream?" I said.

"I don't work in a post office for nothing," she said. "I have my contacts."

She tossed the packet at the bin and it landed with a bull's-eye plop. Anger, it seemed, had propelled her into an Olympic darts player.

Mavis declared to get even.

Getting even seemed to me a bit on the strong side, but seeing Mavis focusing on something other than *Murder She Wrote* on TV was worth any drama. And Mavis hadn't made me tea since the split – not that I ever drank it.

"I know who to speak to," she said and, with her mobile glued to her ear, headed to her bedroom.

The next day she was up before Puss had even thought about food. And she was outside – bra firmly in place – talking to the Roadworks Man, who, at the time, was casually leaning on the "Queue Ahead" sign waiting for the "others" to appear.

Clutching a milky coffee, she tapped him on the shoulder, thrust it into his hand, and asked about the Rod Man.

I watched from the bedroom window as they laughed together, recounting the great sewerage flood at the community centre.

"He's a marvel with a rod," she said.

"Aye, so is your Lumpy."

For a moment Mavis faltered. Her face fell, but soon, with a toot from the postie driving by, Mavis perked up, flashing a smile and a wave.

"I spoke to Sheryl," she said, "she's something else when it comes to DIY."

"So I've heard," muttered the Roadworks Man.

"We just need the plumbing sorted."

She slid a packet of rich tea biscuits from her pocket, peeled it open with as much sensuality as possible with a rich tea biscuit, and smiled.

"My man's your man," said the Roadworks Man, dunking his rich tea.

Mavis was so pleased with herself that she came back with some top-notch coffee for me and the co-op's finest teabags for the workers.

"Steven has offered to do the food," she said. *Although if hard-pressed she could knock up a few egg sandwiches.* "So did Kamal."

"What?" I choked on my coffee.

"But how can you resist Steven's food?" She laughed.

Steven was a man who cooked on par with Sheryl's DIY skills. His food was worth going hungry for. When he talked of bringing "a little something," he meant a spread on par with *Downton Abbey*. Salmon, homemade cake, scones, and cream with flasks of hot chocolate and soup, even a little bubbly for those not driving.

I stared down at the Roadworks Man, who was now working his drill at the side of the road with earplugs in. He looked up and smiled with a thumbs-up. He looked more like a roll and sausage man to me. But I guess spending a weekend installing a hot tub with Steven's posh nosh was way better than spending it alone waiting for the Indian to open.

Then I thought about Kamal and Mavis – and decided not to. Thinking about Kamal always gave me indigestion.

THE GOODBYE

Good goodbyes are rarer than a decent sausage.

The next day Mavis was all geared up and ready to go. It was the middle of summer, which in Scotland means the same as winter: sun, hail, frost, and storms. But also: sunsets at 11pm, sunrises at 4am, and magical moons.

Mavis was out boiling tea with the Bag Lady, and by the time the Rod Man, the Roadworks Man, and Sheryl had arrived, she was handing around cups and having a whale of a time – until that is, her phone rang.

Mavis had spent the morning organising. And for once there was no talk of her sister or Lumpy. Instead, she and Sheryl removed part of the shed and set up the hot tub in there. Sheryl brought her tape measure and gave Betty and the Bag Lady measuring duties while the Rod Man and the Roadworks Man worked on the connections, stopping for as many tea breaks as Steven made.

The hot tub took the best part of a day to fill. And once done, Steven shouted from the kitchen to "come and get it." The smell of scones and soup wafted from the kitchen and we all sauntered in, apart from the Bag Lady. She decided the christening of the hot tub couldn't wait.

The Bag Lady dived in to her tent and reappeared in shorts and a

tee shirt. Her legs were as white as her face was brown. We stared –
hot chocolates suspended – as she flashed across the garden. No one
had seen her legs before.

She slid into the hot tub, disappeared, and then emerged, her tight
bun glistening and her papery brown face laughing. Within minutes
Betty followed. She threw her clothes to the wind and in a red polka-
dot bathing suit disappeared into the water, appearing seconds later
with a wide smile.

The Bag Lady and Betty were surprisingly nimble, which as the
Rod Man put it is "what came from living in a teepee and spending
your evenings sitting by a fire."

The Rod Man and the Roadworks Man stayed until the salmon and
the beer ran out. They took photos of the hot tub for Kamal and
Tenzam and then headed for the Argyll.

"Whenever your drains need unblocking, I'm your man," said the
Rod Man, handing me a parking ticket with a phone number scribbled
on it.

We watched them escort each other down the drive like blood
brothers.

I wondered what their real names were.

No one knew, even Betty, who had served them for years in the
Argyll had no idea.

"I knew a Rod once," she said. "An Australian from down under."

Betty laughed as she recited a joke we had all heard before until the
Bag Lady asked her stop.

Steven jumped with a "time to leave" mutter.

Betty's "down under" joke often had that effect on people.

Steven and Sheryl escorted each other down the drive talking of
which excuse was the most convincing to avoid visiting Sheryl's
mother the next day. Beatrice, Sheryl's mother, was on par with
Mavis's, and they frequently argued over who had the worse.

"Shall we just tell her we can't be arsed?" said Steven as they headed
around the corner.

Sheryl's chuckle rang through the air as Mavis's phone rang.

Her shoulders slumped, her face dropped, as the garden fell silent.

"I see," she said; her voice wavered. "Thank you."

She looked at me with a blank face.

"The nurse said I should come."

I took Mavis. We drove in silence, Mavis now and then wiping her eyes. We entered the hospital and made for the ward. Her sister walked out looking angry.

I was surprised at how much they looked alike. They had the same apple-like figure and round face. Fanny, however, looked hard, with sharp brown eyes like her mother's, while Mavis's eyes were soft and grey. In fact, along with her famed scarf twirling, I thought they were her best feature, delicious to look at. Fanny on the other hand had a glare that could freeze a lake.

She flashed one at Mavis.

"You're too late," she said. "She's gone."

Mavis let out a howl from deep inside. It filled the room, and no one noticed.

I held Mavis hard against my chest to stop her from falling; she howled again, and I held her tighter as Fanny disappeared back into the room.

A trolley crashed about the corridor, a phone rang, a woman answered, and the world carried on as Mavis's hot tears splashed onto my shirt.

There was nothing I could say.

Mavis spent a long time in the other room with her sister. I heard hushed whispering but little else, when she came out I handed her sweet tea. She took one sip, then left it on a ledge and went back into the room for more whispering.

Finally, we left.

I had known Mavis a long time and she had never talked of a sister. Now as I drove her back I knew why. Her sister smouldered anger.

I focused on the road ahead, now and then looking at my pal's crumpled flat face.

"Hate hospital tea," she muttered.

"Who doesn't," I said.

"And McDonald's."

"Me too."

"Mum wanted to die at home, not on a hospital bed."

I was about to say "Who doesn't" again, but when I saw a tear trickle down her face, I handed her a tissue. She blew her nose hard, coughed, and talked of how much she was gagging for coffee.

"The only place open *is* McDonald's," I said.

She said nothing, and when I pulled into McDonald's, she didn't even notice.

I ordered her a coffee, sweet and milky. Without even a glance she placed it in the cup stand of the car, and as I pulled into my drive she silently lifted it and walked into the cottage. By the time I had locked the car she was in her room with Puss on her bed, loudly sniffling.

"Goodnight," I said.

She sniffled.

"You okay?"

"Thank you for the coffee."

"It's a McDonald's," I said.

"I know, thank you."

I made to go.

"She fell asleep," said Mavis, "and never woke up."

"I see."

"Last night."

"I'm sorry."

"Fanny forgot to tell me."

Chapter Thirty-One

JAMES BOND AND MORE

Accept what you feel; it's your secret.

The day Mavis's mother's doctor told her that she had a year at the most, she, according to the carer, snapped. She decided to shock, annoy, and behave badly. She spent her last year wearing odd socks, eating chocolate, and demanding chilli in every-thing – then spitting it out and saying it was too hot.

"I want to experience everything like never before," she said. "I want to piss people off and a noisy funeral. No hymns, just Neil Diamond and Mavis swinging her scarf."

She even wrote it in her will:

"Mavis must dance, or I will come back and curdle your cream, swell your bunions, and haunt you like there's no tomorrow."

The doctor said it was the drugs talking. Fanny blamed her demen-tia, while Mavis hadn't a clue about any new will until her mother died. She was stunned into pensive confusion.

Cat hated Mavis's dancing, and had told her that her apple-shaped body was not "fit for public consumption."

"She was always telling me to stop showing off and cover up," said Mavis. "My mother thought showing off was on par with stealing from a baby. She said my 'middle-aged wobbly stomach would make people sick.' And no matter how many times I told her belly dancing was not about the stomach, she didn't listen."

Mavis, like me, was standing in her dressing gown, staring into the remains of last night's bonfire. She was still reeling from the death of her mother the night before, and I was still in my listening "best friend" mode.

"One night," said Mavis, "Mum was watching an old James Bond film when a belly dancer with a mile-high beehive shimmied onto the screen. "You're too old for that," Mum says and then starts waffling on about harems and paying for things. I tried to tell her that that was not belly dancing, but did she listen? All she was interested in was the tassels and how they 'defied gravity.'"

Mavis tossed the remains of her tea onto the ashes. "At which point I, as usual, stormed off."

The Bag Lady tutted from inside her tent – it was loud enough to prick the ears of Puss, who was loitering about the back door.

"God knows what she meant by 'paying for things,'" muttered Mavis.

I rubbed the sleep from my eyes and yawned.

It was early, none of us had slept. After Mavis went to bed, I sat in the kitchen watching the rain pour onto the Bag Lady's teepee. I could hear Mavis talking on and off to Puss, until I could take no more and knocked on her door.

"You fancy a hot drink?" I said. "The rain has stopped, and I think I can hear Herself."

Four coffees later we were standing by the hot tub listening to the Bag Lady rummage in her teepee. Mavis and I with mugs poised watched as she appeared, head first, followed by a "that'll do" to Puss." Puss had been rubbing herself along Mavis's legs, and the moment she saw the Bag Lady's head appear she was up on her shoulders rubbing whiskers to cheek.

The Bag Lady feigned displeasure – stifling a chuckle.

I looked at Mavis's face, drawn and puffy from crying. She looked small, childlike, and pensive.

When I first met Mavis, she was working in the post office, makeup-less and lonely looking. She didn't even pluck her eyebrows –

belly dancing had changed all that. She discovered purple, glitter, and better bras. Now here she was again, eyebrows unplucked, facial hair sprouting above her lip, looking sad and confused – but at least she was no longer alone.

I watched her hair ruffling in the wind as we waited for the Bag Lady to make herself comfortable and take her tea. The Bag Lady, however, was making a great show of being disturbed – muttering and tutting like there was no tomorrow, pretending to look for Puss's food like I never fed her.

"Why does she want me to belly dance?" said Mavis. "To make a fool of me?"

The Bag Lady grabbed her tea from Mavis. "Not everyone can make a scarf work," she said. Then, with a loud grimace, she jumped onto the swing chair hanging under the only tree in the garden.

She missed.

The Bag Lady and Betty had put it up months ago and regularly fought over who could sit/swing on it.

"It's a talent like any other," said the Bag Lady, going for a second jump.

She missed and with an eye on her tea scrambled to her feet. She handed the mug to Mavis.

Third jump lucky, the Bag Lady positioned herself and then motioned Mavis for her tea. She brought the tea to her lips and was just about to sip when Puss jumped onto her lap, knocking half her tea onto the grass.

I stifled a grin and looked at Mavis – for a moment she smiled.

The Bag Lady, with a casual "I'll pretend that didn't happen" tut, lifted the now half-empty mug to her mouth and sipped it like an alcoholic's first drink. Puss pushed her head under the Bag Lady's other hand.

"You only get to die once," she said with a heavy pat on Puss's head. Puss grimaced. "May as well make a meal of it, ruffle a few feathers."

"Maybe she just wanted something no one would forget," I said.

Mavis sipped her tea. "Who cares, I don't. Fanny is in charge and there isn't a hope in hell of her letting me do anything show-off-ie." She looked disappointed.

"You never know," I said.

"She said my belly dancing would go down like a stink bomb in a perfume factory."

"And there, my little cupcake, is your answer," said the Bag Lady, handing her empty mug to a confused Mavis.

Chapter Thirty-Two

THE PLANNING

Taking control is not always the answer.

Mavis was told on the phone where and when her mother's funeral would take place. She was told in my kitchen while I was whipping up an omelette for us both. I tried not to listen but couldn't help myself.

We had spent the day with the Bag Lady and Betty.

The Bag Lady began talking about fish for tea, which I couldn't face while Betty suggested crisps, which after a few wines led to more crisps and indigestion.

Mavis didn't seem to care, and Betty talking about her husband's funeral didn't help.

"It's important," she said, "to say goodbye as you would want."

Mavis stared into her empty glass. "Fanny has it all under control."

"She's your mother too," said Betty.

"Fanny has always had her way."

"What's happened to you?" I said.

Mavis said nothing.

The Bag Lady offered her the swing chair and dumped Puss on her lap.

"Where's that dancer who sorted out the rugby club?" I said.

Mavis, tight-lipped, stroked Puss. "Mum and Fanny were very close

– it's always been like that. Sometimes, I would be sitting at the table with them and they would forget I was there."

"How could anyone forget you?" said Betty.

"Once we were in a restaurant and they ordered while I was at the loo – without even asking. I was given a plate of liver, *which I hate*, because Fanny said I looked peaky."

Mavis drained her glass.

"So why should it be any different now?"

"Did you eat it?" said the Bag Lady.

"No, I walked out, living up to my drama-queen reputation." She smiled at the Bag Lady. "After I drank my wine."

I looked at Mavis listening to her sister on the phone with a blank look. She was standing in the kitchen blocking the cupboard I needed into.

"I thought she wanted to be cremated," Mavis said.

"That was the dementia talking," said Fanny.

I could hear her precise voice through the phone – once I stopped beating the eggs.

"I don't understand," said Mavis. "Mum never went to church."

"It's not for you to understand," said Fanny.

I tossed the chillies into the frypan along with some onions and peppers – waited for the sizzle and then moved it from the hot plate, so I could hear.

"Mother changed her mind all the time at the end," said Fanny. "Believe me, I know what I am doing, and I know what she really wanted."

I began to beat the eggs again – this time like a madman. Fanny didn't believe in dying wishes; she had said yes to everything when her mother was alive, and now it had all changed.

Mavis hung up as I began to fry on a way-too-hot plate.

"I am going down tonight," she said. "Fanny wants me to help with the catering, apparently my egg sandwiches will make all the difference."

"I'll take you," I said, tossing the egg mixture into the pan.

"Thanks," said Mavis as she headed to her room to pack. I watched her walk, her back slumped like it used to before she learnt to belly dance.

I felt for her; when my mother died I organised it all with my father, and when my father died I organised it all with his sister. We did it together and somehow the sharing helped.

It had all been taken from Mavis and she didn't seem to care. I wondered if she was still in shock. Then I looked back to find my omelette had stuck to the pan.

Chapter Thirty-Three

THE SECRET: PART TWO

You only get to die once.

The takeaway was busy when I walked in. I was late.

I drove back from the care home so relieved I didn't have to stay that I decided to celebrate with a quick walk about the top of Loch Lomond and a latte. By the time I got to the takeaway, it was open and Tenzam was in the kitchen, frazzled while frying. There had been a rush on pakoras, the dips had run out, and the Roadworks Man was getting in the way trying to help. He was searching through the kitchen asking annoying questions.

"Is this the spiced onions?"

"No, that's pickle."

"Shall I put that in a tub then?"

"No, it's twice the price. Kamal will kill me."

"What about this then?"

"That's tandoori."

"Oh."

"It's for marinating, just put it in the back – no I said in the…look, give it here and get some lids."

"Where's the lids then?"

"Under the desk."

"Where?"

"Forget it."

"Are they in the storeroom?"

"No, the desk is out the front."

"The front? Where?"

"Look, don't bother, I can manage, just wait by the phone and answer it."

"Oh, can I not fry something?"

Tenzam manipulated the Roadworks Man to the desk at the front of the restaurant – then he saw me and his round face lit up. He almost kissed me.

"Please sit," he said to the Roadworks Man, marching him to his table.

The Roadworks Man looked disappointed. "I found the lids," he muttered, breaking from Tenzam.

"Just sit," said Tenzam, pushing him back into his seat.

The Roadworks Man glumly picked up the remote, flicked through a few channels, and sighed.

Lumpy entered and Tenzam with a "keep the child entertained" look at him returned to the kitchen.

Lumpy asked for a naga.

"Do you need the tandoori for that?" shouted the Roadworks Man.

Tenzam turned up the radio.

The Roadworks Man with a glare at me lifted the *Fyne News* from the desk, and with a loud scraping of his chair he sat down and started to flick through the paper with vengeance.

I, flashing a look back, lifted the lids from under the desk and started lining them up with the bottoms.

The Roadworks Man continued to flick.

I pulled the spiced onions from the fridge and began to fill the containers.

"I'll have one of them with my naga," said Lumpy.

The Roadworks Man tutted.

Ignoring the extra-loud tut, I began to tell Lumpy about my "second encounter" with the sister, and how I had spent the day rummaging about a small en suite room in a care home while the sisters argued.

"Everything is en suite these days," muttered the Roadworks Man.

"How could two women who look so alike be so different," I said.

"I know," said Lumpy.

The Roadworks Man paused at the article about the bookshop's grand opening. He stopped tutting and began to read...

It had been a trying sort of morning, which I spent making tea and sourcing hot rolls while Mavis was told what to do. She spent her time packing her mother's clothes in the wrong box. Mavis boxed by colour and Fanny wanted it boxed by size. And as Mavis filled the boxes Fanny took them out.

Fanny looked pleased with herself; Mavis looked pissed off.

"Mum would have liked it," she said, "giving all her stuff away."

"You think," said Mavis.

"Of course."

"Don't you think we should wait see how we feel, your daughter might want some of these things, maybe the carers."

"No," said Fanny.

"What do you mean no," said Mavis. "Mum liked the carers."

Fanny stopped folding and looked at her sister. "Mum knows –" She stopped and sighed. "I mean, knew, how I felt about the state of the world, and she gave me carte blanche with regards to her" – she gestured about the room – "things. And that's what I am doing. There are plenty of homeless people with no clothes – out there."

"And a pashmina is going to help?" said Mavis.

"It might."

"Can't we just take a breather and reminisce?"

"Mum wasn't the sort," said Fanny.

Neither noticed Heather, the carer, as she came in to "sort the bed," until Fanny told the Heather "how Mother liked it." The carer argued, telling Fanny how their mum really liked her bed – which riled Fanny into a temper.

"We don't pay you to tell us what our mother so-called liked," she said.

"You don't pay me, the council does," snapped Heather, until Mavis pointed out that her mother was no longer sleeping in the bed and perhaps they should just wash the sheets. At which point both Heather and Fanny burst into tears.

"What would you know, you were never here," Fanny said, blowing her nose.

Then Mavis burst into tears. "Who do you think brought her all those Neil Diamond CDs?"

Heather handed Mavis a tissue and told her how much Mavis's mother liked Neil Diamond. "Maybe you should belly dance to that," she said.

"Belly dancing – there'll be none of that," said Fanny.

"That's what she wanted," said Heather.

"She had dementia," said Fanny. "What would she know about what she wanted?"

"She still watched James Bond," said Heather, "every rerun – she knew them all. Your mother is the only person I know who got excited about Roger Moore. Had no time for Daniel Craig though, said he had Botox. And any man who injects his face as far as your mother was concerned was no man."

Heather and Mavis both laughed until Fanny told the carer that she was talking bollocks.

Heather then pulled a face and started shoving the sheets into the basket like it was a punch bag, then pushed past Fanny with a glare.

"She liked you," muttered Mavis.

Heather stopped and looked at Mavis. "She wanted you to dance." Then she pulled a face, gestured to Fanny, and mouthed, "to piss her off."

I left soon after, grateful for the excuse of the takeaway. Fanny was an uncomfortable woman to be around.

The Roadworks Man sipped his tea with exaggeration and then stabbed at the paper with a poppadum. "It says here she made a mint." The Roadworks Man looked at me. "They broke the Mid Argyll raffle record."

"Is there such a thing?" said Lumpy.

I shrugged my shoulders. "Must be."

"It also mentions your hot tub and..." The Roadworks Man, paused, blushed, and shut the paper. "Mrs Campbell's put in a complaint."

"She always complaining," said Lumpy. "What is it this time – potholes, squirrels nicking underwear, flat beer at the Argyll?"

"The raffle," said the Roadworks Man.

Mavis came home the next day in a mixture of moods. She caught the bus and spent most of it squashed between the window and "some yob" listening to comedy and breathing hangover fumes.

"It was so loud I swear the driver could hear it," she said. "And despite it not being funny, he, the yob, snorted, laughed, and belched from Arrochar to Inveraray and then fell asleep snoring – with the comedy still playing!"

The Bag Lady was sitting at the table; she was reading the *Fyne News* and didn't even notice Mavis. Normally, she would have made a comment or asked for tea, but today she was engrossed in the same bookshop article that the Roadworks Man had been reading.

"I mean since when did young people snore?" muttered Mavis more to herself than anybody.

I told Mavis that perhaps, at the moment, even Betty slipping on a tomato would not make her laugh. The Bag Lady chuckled.

Mavis said little as she struggled with a suitcase. It was extra large and seemed extra heavy. She abandoned it by the table and looked about for a drink.

Mavis had spent the night with Fanny and looked exhausted.

"I always feel so invisible when I am with her," said Mavis.

"How can you say that – you're so colourful," I said.

"That's what Lumpy used to say," she sniffed. "Fanny wants to give everything to charity. She wants to sell Mum's jewellery and send the proceeds to some village in Africa. I didn't know she had anything worth selling. Mum wasn't the sort. I told Fanny she'd be lucky if she got enough for a couple of packets of rice, and she walked out calling me flippant."

I looked at what the Bag Lady was reading. I got as far "'It's all thanks to the book centre committee,' said Amanda," and she closed the paper. She blushed, something I had never seen before, then raced off with the paper under her arm, mumbling something about how Betty would like to see this.

Mavis shut the door behind. "Wonder what's up with her?"

"I have no idea," I muttered as the Bag Lady disappeared into the teepee.

Mavis gestured to the suitcase. "This is from Mum," she said. "Fanny kept it aside."

"Fanny?"

"I know," said Mavis.

"Nice case," I said.

"And it weighs a ton, just about did the driver's back in." We both looked at it.

"Wonder what's in it?" I said.

Mavis made me coffee just the way I liked it before heading to her room.

I stared out at the Bag Lady and Betty in the garden; they were cleaning the hot tub. It was one of those surreal summer evenings where it hardly gets dark and I had a perfect view of the two of them. I was just about to shout at them something bossy about leaving the cleaning till the morning when Amanda appeared. She stood at the edge looking disgruntled and nothing like the chirpy Amanda I knew.

She let out a nervous cough.

"I know what you did," she said.

Betty and the Bag Lady stopped in their tracks. "Don't know what you're talking about," muttered the Bag Lady.

"And if my husband finds out you'll be mincemeat," said Amanda.

Chapter Thirty-Four

THE PLANNING

A man sweats, a woman glows and a cat will lick either.

Fanny took the death of her mother with great drama and coasted through the next week with tears. She told Mavis everything was organised and didn't need her help, then told everyone that Mavis didn't help and she had to do everything. Mavis didn't bat an eyelid. Since the suitcase night, she seemed in a different place.

The funeral was arranged for the end of the week. Five days after Mavis's mother died, Cat was lying in a church she never went to, in a coffin covered in lilies. The scent filled the church, which was full except for Mavis.

The crowd were mostly elderly, sporting a variety of walking aids and coughs, along with a few carers in uniform, two toddlers with no understanding of "stop it," "be quiet," or "sit down," and one teenager with headphones on.

Fanny sat in the front, in between her son and daughter – each with a protective shoulder nudged against hers.

I sat in the middle pew with Lumpy, polished and suited, on one side and a very elderly woman on the other, a large-chested lady who sat with her hands clasped under her chest and let out a volley of throat-clearing, coughing, and a "pardon me it must be the weather" mutter.

The Bag Lady and Betty were sitting at the back – "just in case," said the Bag Lady, "I have to go a place." At the time I didn't suspect a thing, although they both looked like two children waiting to do something they shouldn't. But then they always looked like that.

"Where is Mavis?" said Lumpy.

I had no idea. Last time I saw Mavis she'd been engrossed in photos of her mother and talking in riddles.

Lumpy sighed. "I hope she hasn't planned anything stupid. I mean, there is a time for everything, which Mavis has never grasped."

"Thought that's what you like about her," I whispered.

He didn't answer but smiled a little.

The church was silent except for the organ playing a selection of Neil Diamond tunes. Beside the coffin was a life-size picture of her, twenty-ish in her tennis dress, posing on a tennis court with a man unknown. And on the coffin was her as a teenager with a fifties-style hairdo, looking over her shoulder like a red-haired Elizabeth Taylor.

We waited for Mavis to arrive. The organist finished a prolonged "Sweet Caroline" and looked at Fanny, who motioned to keep playing.

The cougher next to me began to hum and abruptly stopped as an attendant shuffled up to Fanny.

"We have a christening in an hour," he said in an embarrassed whisper *which everyone could hear.*

Fanny looked about the crowd with a lost face. "She should be here," she muttered, as the organist with a stoical stance moved onto "I Am…I Said."

I thought about Mavis and her suitcase. Her light was on for a long time, even after Amanda had left. I'd never seen Amanda in trim like that before, and by the time I decided to go out and investigate, she was giving the Bag Lady a rollicking.

"You all right," I shouted from the kitchen.

"Yes, we're just going to the teepee," said the Bag Lady.

"No need to come out," said Betty.

The Bag Lady with great ceremony opened the teepee and summoned Amanda in; she huffed and bowed her head to enter.

I have never been in the *tent* – ever. And it's not like I haven't asked. But whenever I have, I've received a curt "Not just now," leaving me feel that there would never be a "now" for me.

I wondered why Amanda? What had she got that I hadn't? In fact, what had Betty got that I hadn't? She'd been in the tent more times than Mavis had been in my tea collection.

I went outside. I could hear Amanda talking about her husband.

"He's away," she said. "And I want this mess sorted out by the time he comes back."

"You all right in there? You want anything?" I rattled at the flap.

Betty poked her head from the teepee, nodded to Mavis's bedroom window. "Her light's still on, think she's okay?"

I stared up at the lit window.

"Maybe she could use a drink," shouted the Bag Lady from the back.

I brought Mavis a tea with extra sugar and a ginger snap on the side.

I slipped into her room, placed it on the bedside table, and looked about the room. The floor was covered in photos and on the bed were a few letters and papers.

I picked up a photo of Mavis and her mother. Mavis, an angry-looking teenager, glared into the camera with her mother rigidly posing in a bikini beside her.

"That was taken on a holiday," said Mavis. "Mum stopped me from entering the dance contest. I had to look after Fanny."

I picked up the photo beside it, Fanny standing by a goat, on the verge of tears.

"The carer encouraged Mum to make a memory box," said Mavis "and Mum wanted me to have it. She even left me a note...

"Fanny throws out everything (which you probably know by now). Not like your father, he even kept empty crisp packets. This is for you and don't tell your sister."

She ran her finger across the note.

"I never understood Mum."

Heather gave a small talk about a young Cat who as a child "won enough tennis trophies to fill a bookcase."

"Never be afraid to think outside the box, she used to say." She laughed nervously. "She was my inspiration, she's the reason I took up boxing."

There was an uncomfortable shuffle amongst many of the congregation. Heather's thinking outside the box had led to an affair with a gym manager along with a free subscription, an outrageous hairdo, and matching tattoos. Tattoos that had many asking her to give them "a show."

I wondered where Mavis was.

Fanny stood up next with a speech about her mother managing as a young widow. She looked different to the Fanny at the hospital, smaller, with little makeup and puffy, tearful eyes.

"Never knew my father," she said, "but Mum always talked of him – even said I was like him." She forced a smile. "I wanted to be like her. Well, not when I was a child, as a child I wanted to be anything but like her. I fought with her. I mean she drove me crazy. It was only years later I understood she wanted the best for me."

Fanny looked at her children.

"When I had children of my own." She dabbed her eyes.

The lady next to me coughed. "Pardon me, is this not the christening then?"

Fanny slipped on her glasses and began to read...

"My mother met my father and gave up everything. She took to the farm like a...sorry, can't read my writing, um...so...I...no, she..."

She paused and wiped her eyes again; a few in the congregation coughed.

"But then my mother embraced everything with wide arms and a large dram."

Fanny looked up with a watery smile.

"And the farm was no different. She milked the cows and kept it all going long after my father died, even developed a prize-winning cheese for...um...sorry...goats." Her voice wavered; she paused, looking about the room, and her face crumpled.

"My mother was an inspiration for me," Fanny sniffled. "My first face cream was named after her – the Cat's Milk, wonderful for threaded veins."

Fanny burst into uncontrollable tears, followed by her daughter.

"But I had to change the name..."

"Mum," said the daughter.

Her son stood up and wrapped a protective arm around her.

Her daughter joined them. "You don't need to say anymore," she said.

The organ began to play "Done Too Soon." Fanny, now crying, was led to her seat by her children.

Mavis took a few sips of her tea and a nibble on her ginger snap, then said she was going outside to see how the cleaning of the hot tub was "panning out."

"They have finished," I said. "Having a powwow with Amanda now."

"With Amanda, that's even better."

"Better? How? What do you mean?"

"Amanda's good at things."

"What about me?"

"We all have our own talents," said Mavis with a wistful look. "That's what Mum says."

"When did she say that?"

"Or was it Kamal?"

"Kamal?" I nearly choked on my coffee. When were you speaking to that man?"

Mavis didn't answer but patted my cheek.

"Well," I said, "you're wasting your time, they are in the tent."

"Tent?"

"Yes."

Mavis's face brightened. "With Betty?"

"Yes."

"That's even better."

"So, there is no point in you wasting your time...*better*, what do you mean *better*?"

Mavis, ignoring me, headed for the back door.

"They won't let you in," I said.

Mavis headed into the garden and shouted, "Yoo-hoo, anybody home?"

"You may as well come back inside," I yelled.

Next thing the teepee flap opened and light flooded the garden, like the appearance of an angel.

I waited for them to turn her away; instead an arm reached out and gestured her in, like the arm of the frigging angel.

Mavis disappeared inside, followed by a few feminine coos and a "How you doing, honey?" from Amanda.

"Whose garden is it anyway," I snapped at Puss, who had been standing by her bowl the whole time. She looked up at me and meowed.

I filled her bowl and stared at the tent glowing with light.

"Anyone need anything?" I shouted from the kitchen.

"We're fine," shouted the Bag Lady, followed by a ripple of laughter, and then, from nowhere, James Bond theme music began to blare.

"That's perfect," whispered someone.

The next morning over toast and coffee, Mavis talked in riddles that had me wondering about her sanity.

"That teepee is inspirational," she said with a loud slurp of her coffee.

"I wouldn't know, would I?"

Mavis sighed. "Pure inspirational."

I stared at the teepee – now quiet. Puss stood at the flap and pawed it. The flap opened, and she went in.

"And what's with the James Bond music?" I said.

Mavis refilled her coffee and then mine. "I see things differently now," she said.

"And where did she get the sound system from?" I muttered.

Mavis slapped another dollop of butter on her toast.

"Last night I was moved by many things," she said. "The Bag Lady said it's all about flow. Amanda said I should allow the flow to run its course. And Betty, well, she talked about healing-time and all sorts of things. And she would know, wouldn't she? Her being a widow and all. Do you know what she said?"

Mavis pointed her knife at me; honey dribbled onto her plate.

"Revenge is like medicine."

Mavis ladled what was left onto her toast and licked the knife.

"I'm surprised you heard anything over that racket," I said. "I mean how loud do you need –"

"Stop the flow and you stump emotions, they become strangulated like blocked water..."

"Strangulated?"

"That's what she said...or was it the Bag Lady?"

"How would I know? I wasn't there."

Mavis stared out into the garden. "My sister says she's on high doses of essential oils for anxiety."

"Your sister?"

"Yes, she says she's depressed."

"If you can't feel depressed when your mother dies, when can you?" I said.

"She said she feels overwhelmed."

"Overwhelmed? She was clearing out like a maniac when I saw her."

"She's very extreme," said Mavis. She bit into her toast. "I always thought they were thick."

"Who?"

"My mum and my sister."

"Weren't they?"

"Well yes, that's what I thought, until last night."

❋

When I left with Lumpy for the funeral, Mavis had already gone. I walked into her room, and all the photographs and papers were cleared away except for one lying on her bed.

Mavis had spent the days before the funeral sorting what was in the suitcase. She put all the photos in date order and then the papers and notebooks. Every time I walked into her room it was even more of a mess, with her preoccupied and busy.

Now the bedroom was tidy with only a solitary picture of Mavis when she performed for the home where her mother stayed, posing in her favourite purple belly-dance costume. She had her arms around two ecstatic-looking elderly men, and scrawled at the bottom of the photo were two signatures.

Our Inspirational Mavis – love Eddie and Hamish.

"I took that photo," Lumpy said with a smile.

Chapter Thirty-Five

THE CRY

A Zaghareet is the celebration cry of a belly dancer and has the ability to break an eardrum.

The organist began Neil Diamond's "Cherry Cherry" as the offering plate was passed around. I took one last look about for Mavis. I could not believe that she had missed her own mother's funeral. It was so not like her, and I was beginning to feel like something terrible had happened when a Zaghareet blasted through the air.

The organist stopped mid "Cherry Cherry" as the offering plate crashed to the floor. Everyone apart from the teenager still wearing earphones turned to see who was screaming like a banshee.

"What the hell was that," muttered the old lady beside me.

"The cry of a belly dancer," sighed Lumpy.

"Yalla yalla hey..." echoed again.

I knew that cry anywhere.

Mavis had only once let out a cry like that. It was at a belly dancing gala, and it ruined any chance of us winning. I told her the cry of a belly dancer was meant to be a celebration, not a war cry.

"Try to put more happiness into it," I said. "You sound like you're about to destroy a village."

Then, before we had a chance to breathe or sigh or the organist finish her "Cherry Cherry" rendition, Mavis let out another even louder yell.

"Yalla yalla *hey!*" Her voice echoed around the church.

Fanny stood up and glared at the entrance, she motioned for the organist to start playing. The organist didn't notice; she, like most of the congregation, had never heard anything like it before.

Fanny peered at the door. "Mavis?"

"Yalla yalla hey!"

Mavis appeared at the entrance, the sun silhouetting her frame. She looked like an Egyptian queen covered in purple scarves with gold jewels glittering beneath. It was a spectacular sight of mystery. Mavis's face was covered apart from her Cleopatra-painted eyes.

She posed, allowing everyone to take in her costume, and then began an impressive twirling of her hands – like a flamenco dancer – as her coin bracelets rattled in the silence.

Of course, I had no idea Mavis had something planned. It was Kamal that threw me, and the hot tub.

The night after Mavis's powwow in the teepee, I came home expecting to find Mavis in her room – sorting. Instead she was sitting by the hot tub with a pair of zills in her hand, Betty shouting "one more time" from the tent, and the Bag Lady drumming outside.

When they saw me they stopped...

I had spent the night standing in an empty restaurant, apart from the Roadworks Man and Amanda ordering pakoras for one. Her husband had left due to ongoing moving problems. She didn't even look at the pakoras but instead spent an hour telling me how she'd be lost without such a wonderful man, with not a smile let alone a laugh. And it was only when Lumpy asked her about the raffle that she abruptly left, muttering, "nobody listens to Mrs Campbell."

Mavis playing her zills to the stars was the last thing I expected to see.

The shed was perfect for the hot tub. Sheryl had built a veranda around it which was big enough for the coal scuttle fire and the Bag Lady to play her music on – which she was now doing.

When I first met the Bag Lady it was the electric organ and the same song. Now it was a small drum and the same beat – accompanied by the James Bond theme playing from the teepee.

"You're home early," said the Bag Lady.

"There was no one apart from Amanda," I said.

The Bag Lady shifted uncomfortably and muttered something about the husband "not being all he's cracked up to be."

Betty switched off the music and came out of the teepee. She looked at me. "You're back early."

"Yes, so it seems," I said, feeling not for the first time like an unwanted teacher/partner/parent in my own garden.

"We're just studying the sky," said Mavis. "It's been a long time since I've stared at the stars."

"The stars know everything," said the Bag Lady.

"Hear, hear," muttered Betty.

"I have spent a lifetime under them," said the Bag Lady. "They see all."

"My husband didn't believe in the stars," said Betty. "He said horoscopes were for losers. Bet he feels stupid now."

"My Mum was a Leo like my sister," said Mavis.

"My mother was run over by the bin lorry," said the Bag Lady.

She stopped drumming...

"In all the time I have known you," I said. "I have yet to hear that one."

"I was brought up by my gran," said the Bag Lady. "In a house the size of a potting shed. She was a woman you didn't want to argue with. All's we had was potatoes and mint... there is nothing I don't know about mint."

"Aye right," I said.

She gestured to the sky. "Every night I'd sit outside that potting shed, look at the stars, and wonder which was my mother. Was she looking down on me?"

"My mum sent me to stay at a farm with an Aunt," said Betty "For a holiday, with a woman who thought milk was good for you and even better when watered down with ginger ale. She lived in the middle of nowhere and ate liver and kidneys." She looked at the Bag Lady "what I wouldn't give for a bit of mint."

Mavis's face fell. "Never got to say goodbye."

Betty patted Mavis's knee. "Aye but you will do something better – bigger."

If only I'd listened.

The Bag Lady gave a few beats on her drum. "This is your chance – be extravagant with your grief."

"And do it with colour," said Betty, who had recently dyed her hair red. "I wore every colour I could to my husband's funeral."

"My sister did though," said Mavis. "She said Mum held her hand and said goodbye, and other things which were" – Mavis sighed – "personal. She wasn't even warm when I touched her...looked serene though."

"You mother looked serene?" I said.

The Bag Lady poked the fire. "It's the stars, what we come from and where we go back to."

Betty nodded.

"That's what Kamal says," said Mavis. She looked at her phone.

"Kamal," I said. "What has he got to do with anything?"

Mavis stood up and went inside.

I followed her.

"Kamal?" I said. "What is he talking about stars for?"

"He likes to talk about his mother too," she said and went back into her room.

The church was quiet; all eyes were on Mavis.

"Mavis?" whispered Fanny.

Mavis nodded at the Bag Lady.

The Bag Lady flicked a switch and disco lights fluttered into action pulsating blue, green, and red behind her silhouette. Mavis's hands circled about her eyes as she looked from one person to the next.

"Jesus," muttered Shifty.

"Jesus has nothing to do with that," coughed the lady next to me.

Betty and the Bag Lady had agreed to help Mavis. It had all been arranged in the teepee; it was the Bag Lady's selection of James Bond music that swung it. That and the fact that her rucksack was the perfect hiding place for my iPod and a portable disco light. Where they got the portable disco light I have no idea, but Fanny, it seems, thought disco was the death of dance – making them an absolute must for Mavis.

Neil Diamond's "Cherry Cherry" was the signal to move into position. As the last chorus began to play, the Bag Lady and Betty, poised by the sockets, were ready to flick the switches.

All was going to plan until Mrs Campbell glanced across the pew and saw the whole reason for her misery...

"I know youse," she snapped.

The Bag Lady flicked the switch.

No one listened; they were still staring at Cleopatra Mavis and her flamingo hands moving to the muffled sounds of James Bond.

"Turn it up," hissed Mavis.

Mrs Campbell, a long-standing cleaner from Lochgilphead, was a woman most tried to ignore. She was an alcoholic famous for shouting in the street at her ex, usually in the middle of the night. She was a renowned complainer, drunk or sober, who ranted at anyone behind a counter. She shouted at the co-op manager about his "buy one, get one free" being out of date. She moaned at Chubby the butcher's steak being as tough as her ex's hide. And she frequently wrote into the "Points of View" section of the *Fyne News*, which most people usually skimmed. She even sent in a three-page rant about the raffle. The editor took one look and cut it down to two paragraphs of "juicy bits."

"I have bought a million of those so-called raffle tickets," Mrs Campbell wrote. "My daughter winning that hot tub was her last hope."

Mrs Campbell's daughter was apparently "at death's door" and was so ill she couldn't make it to the funeral.

"Fat chance of winning with those two con artists rigging the raffle," she wrote. "Is that legal? Can we order a recount?"

No one read the piece apart from Amanda. And now, having spent most of her lunch in the pub next door, Mrs Campbell, bleary-eyed and slurry, glared at the two women. As far as she was concerned, they were the only reason her daughter could not have what she should have.

Mrs Campbell, with the courage of a couple of double whiskies, let out another louder cry.

"Youse are the one that won, if youse can call cheatin' winnin'."

Still no one heard; the Bag Lady had turned up the James Bond theme music to full volume.

Mrs Campbell, exasperated that no one was listening, stood up and with a robust tug of the plug silenced the music.

"Youse are for it, and if youse know what's good for yer you'll sort it."

Betty posed at the electric socket glared back. "You're making up stories, that lottery was fair draw, you ask my Shifty."

"Aye that'll be right," Mrs Campbell shouted and made a grab for Betty's disco ball.

The Bag Lady tugged the disco ball from her.

"We didn't win anything," she said and pointed at me. "She did."

Chapter Thirty-Six

MRS CAMPBELL AND THE DISCO BALL

There is more to a minister than a dog collar.

Like a true professional, Mavis held her standing pose, waiting for her moment.

Lumpy stared spellbound at her, while Mrs Campbell now stared at me. "So you set 'em up – youse are to blame."

"I knew nothing about it," I said.

"It's in her garden," said Betty.

I glared at her, along with everyone in the church, including the teenager, who had pulled his earphones off.

Mrs Campbell moved towards me and stuck her finger in my face. "You look smug right enough."

"Mrs Campbell," said Lumpy, removing her finger from my face. "My friend here works in the takeaway. She has nothing to do with the raffle.

For a minute, Mrs Campbell stopped and looked at me like she had seen me before but couldn't remember where. Then she continued her rant.

"My daughter has MS," she shouted, looking about the congregation. "A curry's the last thing she can eat."

The minister looked at Fanny and gestured to his watch...

Fanny turned to Mrs Campbell. "Your ruining my mother's funeral."

"That hot tub was hers," hissed Mrs Campbell.

"The christening," said the minister.

Mavis dropped her pose and turned to Mrs Campbell. "How many whiskies have you had?"

"Oh, it's the postmistress," coughed the woman next to me.

It never occurred to me that the Bag Lady and Betty had done anything suspicious. I was too concerned about Mavis and her frequent references to Kamal.

I kept trying to warn her, but did Mavis listen? The only advice she listened to was the Bag Lady and Betty telling her to "throw caution to the wind." I had no idea they were talking about the funeral.

I thought they were talking about men – encouraging her to "throw caution to the wind" with Kamal. A man from whom you should draw up the drawbridge, lock the gate, and swallow the key. A man best avoided, who made loneliness a godsend. And I told this much to Mavis, not that she listened. Now I wished I'd listened to her instead. Maybe I could have stopped her.

Mrs Campbell staggered, then righted herself. "Just wishing my dear friend the best with a couple of Johnnie Walker's best."

"You're no friend of my mother's," said Fanny.

Mavis walked up to her. "You're just here for the drink."

"What drink? This do is as dry as a Jacob's cracker," said Mrs Campbell with a mild slur.

"This is a church," said the minister, who was starting to look agitated.

Fanny joined her sister. "You don't have to stay."

"Let's have some dignity, ladies," said the minister. "Remember where we are and why we are here."

"Your mum was my pal, even sent my daughter a get-well card." Mrs Campbell forced a few tears and then turned to the woman next to her. "She has IBS you know, she has to watch everything."

"Thought you said it was MS."

"She has both, and it's not easy, and..." She threw another glare at the congregation. "A hot tub," she began to shout, "would've made all the difference" – she paused – "to that dear, dear daughter of mine."

Mrs Campbell stopped, blew into her hankie, and then glared at the Bag Lady with a look of venom. She staggered, looked at Betty's disco ball, then looked back at the Bag Lady and saw the iPod by the wall.

She righted herself.

"Youse the one," she muttered. "Youse the one I saw selling tickets, writing names on the tickets..." Her voice grew louder. "...screwing 'em up in the bag. You, aye youse."

She pointed her finger at the Bag Lady.

"I saw youse with all the tickets. What'd yer do, how'd yer manage it?"

Mavis, seeing her pal about to be at the end of one of Mrs Campbell's famous "slaps across the chops," which was usually meant for "the ex," sprang into action. She grabbed Mrs Campbell's arm.

There was a tussle.

Mavis was strong and overpowered her until her scarves got in the way of her feet. Mavis tripped and skidded and Mrs Campbell grabbed, pushed, and pulled Mavis's scarf from her face.

"Knew it was youse and yer stupid belly dancing."

Fanny jumped in, yelling something about belly dancing taking more balls than Mrs Campbell and her ex had together.

"It's not a dance for the faint of heart," she yelled.

Which for a second stopped Mavis in her tracks – long enough for Mrs Campbell to take advantage. She, with both hands and the force of fifteen stone, pushed. Mavis didn't stand a chance. She went down with a cascade of purple, a clatter of coins, and a yelp.

Lumpy jumped up.

Fanny jumped in with a swift grab at Mrs Campbell's arm. Mrs

Campbell pulled away, swayed, toppled, overcompensated, staggered, and righted herself as her pale blue hat toppled to the ground.

Lumpy made to move and then saw Kamal in the distance.

"What is he doing here?" I said.

"Oh, I forgot," muttered Lumpy. "He's Mavis's taxi."

"Taxi? Him?"

Lumpy sat back down as Kamal came to Mavis's side and was, within minutes, kneeling at her head – on top of Mrs Campbell's blue hat.

"You all right?" said Kamal to Mavis.

And she looked up at him. "Think so."

Mrs Campbell pulled her hat from under Kamal's knee and, with a fair amount of swearing, punched it back into shape and slapped it back onto her head.

Kamal told her to leave; the minister, with a grim face, gestured to the door and began to guide her.

Mrs Campbell at first followed – made for the door and then at the last minute raced for the Bag Lady and past her and made a grab for the iPod.

Fanny went for a lunge, but she overestimated herself and both she and Mrs Campbell fell to the floor. Mrs Campbell's hat rolled by Kamal's feet. He stepped on it, twisted his foot into it, and then dragged it across the floor as he went to help Fanny.

And that's when the real Mrs Campbell took over.

Chapter Thirty-Seven

HEATHER'S DIGNITY

A hat without a head is like a burger without a bun.

Mrs Campbell is a person not to be messed with, especially when it comes to her hats.

She had the speed of a boxer and a left hook that could bring an elephant to its knees. With one punch, she knocked Kamal out and silenced the church.

It took ten minutes for Kamal to come around, and when he did, he saw Mavis's painted Cleopatra face looking into his and whispered, "My Cleo."

Lumpy left soon after that. Without a backward glance at Mavis he grabbed Mrs Campbell, shoved her in the front seat of his car, and, with a small skid, drove off.

I left with Heather the carer. Mavis was by that time sitting by Kamal wiping blood from his nose, and Fanny was on the other side with a packet of wet wipes.

Heather stared at the slashing rain on the windscreen and talked non-stop about Cat. Heather had spent her short working life (she was only thirty) caring for others and thought nothing of it.

She had no idea of the comfort she gave people. She cleaned and joked with those she saw and didn't really bat an eye at things that other people pulled faces at. She had a dignity about her and an ability to bristle about a room unnoticed despite how ill the person. I saw her breeze in and out of Cat's room like daylight. It was a quiet comfort even for me.

"Never seen a dead person," she said. "Let alone watch them die."

"It's not something people like to talk about," I said.

"One minute breathing, next gone." She looked at me as we headed around the roundabout. "I was the last person she talked to before she died."

"Really?" I said.

I looked at her slim face; it was pale, with Elizabeth Taylor makeup and a black bob. Her get-up was just the same as she wore to work. I admired her guts to walk about the way she did. She stood out wherever she went with her fifties look and one tattooed arm. It was a tattoo that demanded a second glance. And, according to her, it had been inspired by one of Cat's thinking-out-of-the-box speeches. People often stopped and asked her about it; the old boys in the home loved it.

A large fish swirled around the length of her left arm with a tail like a showgirl spanning her wrist and fingers, and its large grin covered the outside of her upper arm. There was a cigar balanced on the side of its lips and a wink with extra-long lashes on the other side of its face. As she drove, I stared from the wink to the cigar.

"Well it was not really me she talked to," she said. "It was to her dead husband. She saw him in the corner. And in her more lucid moments she talked about regrets."

"Regrets?"

"Yes, she said she had none."

"She must have felt comfortable with you," I said.

"Do you think?" Heather smiled. "She asked me about the tattoo when I got it."

Most people did.

"I told her it is the fish that got away, or never got caught – depending on the story. I like to think that I almost got caught by the wrong man, the wrong job, but I too got away. Cat loved hearing that."

Heather told stories like a gypsy.

She stopped the car and began to fill it with petrol. I offered to pay but she waved it away, so I bought her a coffee and chocolate instead.

The rain had stopped, and we were halfway home. Heather's driving slowed as she continued to talk.

"In the end she whispered, 'I'm coming,' closed her eyes, and never woke up. By the time Fanny arrived she was unconscious and smiling serenely."

"Serenely?"

"First time I had ever seen her look serene. Don't know what she'd think about the funeral. Never in her wildest dreams would she have imagined that happening."

"A punch-up at her funeral?"

"No, her daughters ganging up together."

She pulled up outside my house and turned to me.

"Fanny was heartbroken when she realised I was the last person Cat spoke to. Don't know why, Cat never said one positive thing to Fanny. But then not many old folk do – do they? Not by the time they get to the home, they're lucky if they remember who their family are. Cat did like to play the sisters off each other. And yet when they weren't there, she talked about them all the time, like she was proud of them."

"And yet she had no regrets?" I said.

"None, well apart from not seeing the coach again."

Mrs Campbell came into the takeaway the day after the funeral. Kamal was standing behind the counter counting up his money. His eye was at the puffed-up-like-a-golf-ball-and-can't-open stage. Every facial move-ment caused him to wince, but then he always was a drama queen.

He looked up to see Mrs Campbell standing with her arms folded across her chest and choked on his tea.

"Where's that Lumpy?" she snapped. "He's got my hat in his car."

"Your hat? What has this to do with me?" He glared at her. "Get out or I'll call the police."

"You owe me," she said and then paused. "I mean he owes me."

"What?"

"For a fucked-up hat. That hat cost a fortune." Mrs Campbell huffed. "You're lucky I'm not going to bother about the hat."

"Now I am lucky – what do you mean? Look at me? What do you think this is?" He pointed to his eye. "A tub of ice cream?"

"No, seriously, you are, that I decided not to go to the police," she said.

Kamal gave a lopsided smirk. "You – what do you mean you? I am friends with Lumpy too, you know."

"Yes, well I just want my hat."

"Lumpy is not here, don't know where he is."

"Try the Chinese," said the Roadworks Man.

Kamal glared at him.

I was just about to ask if she wanted to order something when Mavis and her sister walked in looking like best friends.

Mrs Campbell looked from one face to another. "And youse are no better; your mother would be heartbroken," she said and stomped out with a "that Chinese is way better than this friggin' dump" mutter.

Kamal fluttered a smile at Mavis and an even bigger one at her sister.

"That woman is trying to blackmail me out of free poppadums." He feigned a laugh at Fanny. "As if."

Fanny cooed while Mavis glanced at me.

Chapter Thirty-Eight

THE DANCE OF THE CHILLIES

A curry without a chilli is like a pakora without batter.

A week after the funeral, Kamal's black eye had gone from a swollen pink golf ball to a colourful purple mass. And Fanny and Mavis were on the phone several times talking about a memorial for their mother. The reception had been postponed and neither was sure about what to do next, and for the first time Mavis had a say.

It was hard to tell just how friendly Mavis was with Kamal. But she seemed to be more her old self, not particularly happy or sad but more stoical. She started wearing makeup again, went back to work, and even replaced my sherry – not that I wanted her to.

"I owe you this and more," she said one morning and handed me a bottle of top-of-the-range Spanish sherry.

"There's no need," I muttered. It had been an unwanted raffle prize; I hated sherry, even in a trifle.

"No, I insist," Mavis said.

I looked at her staring into the garden; "Glad to be rid of it" was on the tip of my tongue, but she looked so pensive I didn't have the heart.

"Thank you," I muttered. I slid the next raffle prize offering back into the tea cupboard and poured her a real drink, whisky.

I mean, no one should drink sherry while grieving.

"Don't thank me," she said with a sip. "Kamal recommended it – it's from Tesco's."

Lumpy, on the other hand, seemed to disappear. He stopped coming into the takeaway and took to Chinese. Tenzam was lost; he missed his pal and their talks.

Every night when the door opened, Tenzam's head would pop out from the kitchen with a smile of expectancy and then drop.

"Told you he's not coming back," said the Roadworks Man. "Your man Kamal went too far."

"Kamal is not mine," said Tenzam.

"Just a figure of speech," muttered the Roadworks Man with a shrug.

We all missed Lumpy, even me. The night was so much longer without me trying to get him and Mavis back together.

And making do with the Roadworks Man was not always easy. He took nagging to a new level. He also missed Lumpy, but unlike Tenzam, he habitually pointed it out to the point that even I wanted to tell him to shove a poppadum in it.

"A fine curry. Lumpy would like this."

"A fine film. Lumpy would like that."

"A fine joke. Lumpy would laugh his head off."

In fact, there was nothing that Lumpy would not like, according to the Roadworks Man, and both Tenzam and I began to develop a new code of eyebrow raising, face pulling, and tutting each time the word "fine" was mentioned.

Within one week we had developed a sign language that led to sniggering, and Tenzam even threatened to add extra chillies in the Roadworks Man's dips if he mentioned Lumpy one more time.

Which soon followed with a dance of the chillies – a comic mime created by Tenzam using the chilli in a variety of ways physically impossible in the real world. It was one of the funniest things I'd seen since Puss sniffed cayenne pepper, and it led to both of us sniggering in the kitchen until the Roadworks Man shouted, "What's up with you guys?" – making us laugh even more.

Mavis had been in to the takeaway several times. Tenzam once asked if she had seen Lumpy and was greeted with a curt "Hardly."

Tenzam made her mild dishes that were covered in yogurt. She even came in with her sister once and ordered a mild korma. How a korma can be anything but mild was beyond me. But Tenzam did his best, and when she asked how much he waved his hand.

"Care of Kamal," he said and went back into his kitchen.

The Roadworks Man blew through his teeth. "Freebies, ladies, Lumpy never got one of those."

Which went completely over the sister's head and sent Tenzam into a frenzy of chilli mimes, followed by silent hysteria in both of us.

Amanda came in every night ordering for one. The Roadworks Man asked about her husband several times, but all she did was mumble about the raffle tickets and how she needed to sort things out before he came back.

"I spoke to that Mrs Campbell," said Amanda. "Do you know her daughter doesn't even live here? She's down south; all that rubbish about the hot tub healing her daughter."

"Could have told you that," said the Roadworks Man.

"I said to her, 'How's your daughter going to benefit from a hot tub here when she's down in Norwich?' And do you know what she said? 'She visits as often as she can, being that she is in a wheelchair.'"

"Could have told you that and all," said the Roadworks Man.

She threw the Roadworks Man a look.

"Aye, she's always causing trouble, that woman," said the Roadworks Man. "Tried to get a free carryout with the boss here. She said as he sold the ticket to her that he was liable."

"For what?" I said.

"That's what he said."

Amanda sat down with a slump. "Trouble? That woman has been on the phone in the shop, and at home – where she got my number from I have no idea, but it was the last straw for my husband. He didn't want to come up here in the first place."

"Never force a man to move, he'll only dig his feet in," said the Roadworks Man.

She glared at him. "Is that not heels?" She looked at me. "Now he says it's full of fruit loops and nutcases."

"Lochgilphead, the muesli bowl of Argyll," said the Roadworks Man.

"Wish I never had the goddamn raffle," said Amanda.

In the end, Mrs Campbell moved on to other complaints. Kamal told Fanny and Mavis he'd sorted her out – reached an agreement. He agreed not to complain about the black eye to the police if she stopped making accusations about the raffle tickets. It was a successful agreement sealed with a few free pakoras, so he claimed.

Mavis was so impressed she asked him to come and sample the hot tub.

"Hot tub in Scotland?" he said. "What does your sister think of this?"

And when Kamal asked if her sister would be there, Mavis looked at me, and this time I didn't say a thing.

Chapter Thirty-Nine

ONE CUSTOMER TOO MANY

A meal on your own is rarely treasured.

Kamal appeared a week later on Sunday for the usual money counting; by then his eye was a range of purple shades. He arrived as the Roadworks Man was cleaning his plate with his naan and Amanda was waiting for her pasanda for one. Since the hot tub fiasco, Amanda had taken to all things creamy and full of ghee, a naan with everything, and sometimes even chips.

Amanda had developed a fondness for sitting next to the Roadworks Man with a Coke while waiting. Everything he said she argued with, which inflamed him and seemed to bring a spark to her eyes.

Today she seemed to have a sense of relief about her, and she hadn't even started on her winding up of the Roadworks Man. She eyed the Roadworks Man's empty plate and began to moan about the chippie.

"Their chips are rubbish, full of *scraps* − even the seagulls turned their nose up at them."

"Some say scraps are the best bit," said the Roadworks Man.

"We serve quality here," said Tenzam.

Kamal flicked the till open; the drawer burst forth and Kamal expertly jumped out of the way. The Roadworks Man let out a loud tut as Kamal began to empty the drawer.

"Women aren't worth the loss of a pal," he muttered, a phrase he had muttered to most customers who appeared.

Kamal continued to count.

"Aye, you can a pull a woman any time, but a good pal's hard to find – like hens' teeth," said the Roadworks Man.

"A hen has no teeth," said Kamal.

"Exactly," said the Roadworks Man with a slurp of his tea.

"Met Lumpy the other day," said Amanda. She paused, looking from the Roadworks Man to Tenzam. "In the Chinese."

"I'd be there myself if that place had a table," said the Roadworks Man.

Kamal looked up, glared, and then resumed his counting.

"Food's no good without the right company," said the Roadworks Man.

"I was walking past on my way to Tesco's and there he was ordering a sweet and sour."

"He hates Chinese curry," said Tenzam.

"Apparently that's all he orders these days," muttered the Roadworks Man with a sage look.

"He's only been gone a couple of weeks," I said.

"Is that all?" muttered Tenzam.

"Lumpy is but one customer," muttered Kamal, who began to bag his money.

"He said that driving Mrs Campbell home was the ride of a lifetime, and not in a good way," said Amanda.

"That woman can talk the hind legs off a goat," said Tenzam.

"Donkey," I said.

"Yes, this woman is a pest," Kamal muttered, now counting his bags.

"Lumpy told me that she spent the whole journey home complaining," said Amanda. "After what she did?"

Tenzam handed her her takeaway She peered inside and continued.

"He said she complained about the council, her giro, her credit cards, her bills..."

"Bills?" said the Roadworks Man. "That woman is on every benefit going – what bill does she have, a tick bill at the Argyll? She's even got a blue badge. I mean what the hell does she need one of those for? She's hardly disabled, not when she can punch like a kung fu queen."

"She even complained about the dentist and the crappy music they play," said Amanda. "As well as the doctor's 'stupid appointment system.'"

"She has a point there," muttered the Roadworks Man.

"Then she started to complain about Mavis and the Bag Lady. 'Well,' said Lumpy, 'I told her to stop right there. "Everyone saw you knock a grown man out cold — how do you think that is gonna affect your sickness benefits? If I were you I'd shut my mouth and find something else to complain about."'"

Kamal slammed the till shut and began to dial his phone as he walked into the kitchen. "Mavis, is that you?" he said. "Do you know where Fanny is?"

I heard a muffled Mavis tone along the lines of "why should I?"

"I need to speak with her," he said.

The door opened, and Mavis walked in with her phone to her ear.

"My sister" — Mavis looked at me — "is on the verge of a breakdown."

Kamal tutted. "Well I need her to sort my back, that punch did something — a click — and she needs to sort this."

There was a pause. Mavis walked behind the counter.

"She — you owe me," he said.

"Getting her to agree to anything is like squeezing grapes for juice," said Mavis, now in the kitchen.

"This is possible," muttered Kamal.

"You think?" said Mavis as she tapped him on his shoulder.

Kamal put his phone down. "You and your silly games."

Amanda looked up at me and then continued with her story, which in the end was the final straw for Mavis.

Chapter Forty

THE TENT

The difference between a tent and a teepee is more than spelling.

In the last few weeks, Mavis had spent more time with her sister than she had ever spent since she left home as a teenager. At first, they seemed to bond over the Mrs Campbell incident, until the arrangements for the rescheduled memorial came up. Fanny called the memorial *her* mother's, and Mavis, tight-lipped, suggested they call it a celebration of *their* mother's life.

Their relationship stuttered from talks to silences about the final goodbye of a woman they each remembered differently. Their memories were as separate as they were. Mavis, being ten years older, left when Fanny was still a girl. And neither seemed to want to admit that the only thing they had in common was no longer with them.

After the Mrs Campbell incident, Mavis went back to work. She spent her days silently at the post office and her evenings talking to anyone who'd listen. She sat in the takeaway or outside the teepee asking me my opinion – ignoring it, then asking someone else, usually the Bag Lady.

The Bag Lady for some reason had little to say and instead would drum to the stars, and Mavis would switch of her phone and stare.

One night, Mavis announced to us all by the fire that her sister was now officially a wreck.

"I've asked her to join us and take a dip in the hot tub. I hope you don't mind?"

No one said anything as the fire crackled.

"You have no idea what it's like talking to her about Mum. Fanny talks about the last hours she spent with her like they were a revelation. She said Mum told her everything, although she won't tell me what that 'everything' is. She just bursts into tears and tells me that organising a celebration of her life seems as possible as a Mount Everest climb. The next minute she's looking at food for the buffet. It's like talking to two women. I am out of my depth. In fact," said Mavis, "she should be here any minute."

The hot tub revved into action as we heard a series of toots followed by a silver car reversing up the drive. It was a huge tank-like car that could cause irreparable damage with just the slightest bump and so high Fanny had to jump to get out of it.

It was clean, polished to the max, with a sound system loud enough to fill a stadium. Just like the car Shifty used to drive and my ex wished they still had.

Fanny switched off "Cherry Cherry" and, with a light landing on the gravel, waved.

"Still okay?" she said sheepishly. "I mean, I am not interrupting anything – am I?" She moved to her sister and gave her an awkward rub on the shoulder.

Mavis took her bag inside.

"Thanks," she muttered with a sigh. "It's been a long time since I've stared at the stars in a swimsuit. Mavis says you do it all the time. I can't wait."

"Wait no longer. The sun has sunk and the moon has slid from its bed," said Betty, who had been heavy-handed with the sloe gin.

"The moon doesn't slide," said the Bag Lady. She looked at Fanny. "We all suffer from Betty's idea of poetic wisdom."

"I like poetic wisdom," said Fanny.

Mavis threw me a "she would" look as Fanny plonked herself between Betty and the Bag Lady like they were old friends. The Bag Lady shifted away while Betty shifted closer.

It was a warm summer's night still moist from the day – perfect for midges. Betty, inspired by the clear sky and full moon, began pointing out the stars like she had been to the moon and back and knew each one personally.

We had heard it all before, but Fanny hadn't and sat with a rapt expression, ignoring the pinging from her phone.

The Bag Lady contradicted Betty whenever possible, in between slapping midges that seemed to have zoned in on her.

Betty and the Bag Lady had fallen out over drumming. Betty claiming that the Bag Lady "hogged the drum," while the Bag Lady reminded her it wasn't *the* drum but *her* drum.

Usually a good dose of sloe gin and a splash in the hot tub sorted things. But tonight, thanks to the midges nibbling on the Bag Lady and skipping Betty, it was different. The Bag Lady wanted nothing more than an early night and Fanny egging Betty on wasn't helping.

"Mum loved looking at the stars," whispered Fanny.

"I don't remember her saying anything about the stars apart from horoscopes being bollocks," said Mavis.

"Mother had books on the stars," said Fanny, pulling out her phone.

"Those books were Dad's," said Mavis. She turned to me. "He said animals and stars were connected and it helped him on the farm."

Fanny, now reading her mobile with a pained expression, didn't hear.

"Why don't you turn that thing off?" said Mavis.

Fanny looked hurt, and small. "Could be mother..." She stopped, sniffed, then wiped her nose. "...I mean, one of the children."

For a moment I felt for her.

"They're not children anymore," said Mavis.

"I know," she sighed with another glance at her phone. "But they worry about me."

"Children shouldn't worry about their parents," sniffed the Bag Lady.

"Maybe you're right," said Fanny. "It's just that after everything that's happened, we need each other."

"I understand," said Betty, glaring at the Bag Lady. "I'm a mother too."

The Bag Lady huffed. "I'd hardly call you maternal," she said.

"I'd hardly call you a drummer," said Betty.

Fanny stopped. "You drum?"

The Bag Lady shifted uncomfortably.

Betty pulled the drum from the tent. Fanny began to mutter "awesome" and "fab."

"It's a drum," said Mavis.

Fanny looked at the Bag Lady. "Where did you get it from?"

"A drum shop," snapped Mavis.

"That's not strictly true," said Betty. "It was more *acquired*, shall we say."

Fanny turned the drum around with a rapt, some would say over-the-top, look.

"The beats," she said. "They go well with stargazing, and I find it helps me."

"With what?" said Mavis.

"Saying goodbye. The stars know everything," muttered Fanny.

"Hear, hear," said Betty.

"I wouldn't say they know everything," said the Bag Lady.

Betty choked on her sloe gin. "You say that all the time."

Fanny asked the Bag Lady to play and the Bag Lady smiled.

"I need the right atmosphere." She smacked her neck. "And none of these midges."

"Midges are all in the mind," said Betty. "Why don't you jump in the hot tub?"

The Bag Lady thrust her arm covered in bites under Betty's nose and shouted, "Well what do you call these, oh goddess of the tub?"

"Mere pimples," said Betty. "I have seen bigger bites on a marshmallow..."

"I've some oil for midges," said Fanny.

Betty stopped. "Oil for midges?"

Fanny took the Bag Lady's arm and began to examine with a concerned look. "Yes, and the bites too."

"The bites?" said the Bag Lady. She almost looked impressed.

Then Fanny with a soft delicious voice offered to massage as a thank-you.

For what I have no idea.

"I could do your arms and feet," she said, "it will keep the midges away and heal the bites."

"Heal bites? Really?" said the Bag Lady.

"Yes," said Fanny. She jumped up and headed for her car. Betty and the Bag Lady watched as Fanny returned with her "massage box" which she always brought "just in case."

"You never know when a massage emergency might strike," Mavis muttered as the three women disappeared into the teepee.

We should have gone inside, poured a decent drink, and laughed about it all. But we didn't. Instead we sat glued to our seats, jealous, pissed off, and not the least bit drunk while listening to the women ooh and arrrh like in an old-fashioned porn film.

Just there – that's the spot...

Oh, and just there – a little to the right; no, left; almost there; yes, yes, yes, that's it...

Oooh, again...

Harder...

"How easily we are bought," muttered Mavis.

I stared at the tent. "I haven't been bought in ages," I muttered. "In fact, I can't remember the last time someone tried to buy me" – I topped up our glasses – "and I couldn't give a toss about what's inside that goddamn tent."

Heaven, sighed a voice from the tent.

"Quite right," said Mavis.

Chapter Forty-One

FANNY

Years ago, we foraged in the wood. Now the only foraging we do is for buy-one-get-one-free in the co-op.

The next morning, Mavis and I were sitting in the kitchen when Fanny walked in looking annoyingly fresh.

Fanny had tucked into the sloe gin, the wine, even dabbled in whisky, which, like Mavis, was not a good idea.

Fanny spent ages massaging the two women and followed it up with a lecture about "life's healing choices" in a motherly "I know better than you" voice. In that time Mavis threw more wood on the fire and I opened another bottle of wine. Finally, Fanny appeared with a relaxed Betty and a glowing Bag Lady with not an insect bite in sight.

"Organic is the way to go," she said, "and as for drinking, just remember what I said, alcohol plus midges equals inflammation."

The Bag Lady was so grateful she made Fanny a hot chocolate. Fanny refused until she sipped it and soon, like Mavis, was skipping the hot chocolate and topping up the whisky.

After her first attempt on the swing, we hid the whisky.

Then she moved onto the sloe gin, which apparently her father had left a shed full of after he died.

Fanny never knew her father, but that didn't stop her going on about him. In fact, the sloe gin seemed to have erupted a volcano of emotion in Fanny on par with Mrs Campbell.

Mavis and Fanny's father was a farmer who not only looked after sheep but loved them. He even left a loft full of pictures of them which Fanny cleared out and had been "tortured by the experience" ever since.

Mavis called her a drama queen, which the Bag Lady thought was a bit steep, until Fanny made a second jump for the swing and shouted, "Where the fuck do you think I got my name from?"

"I thought it was a famous thing," muttered a disillusioned Betty. "*Fanny by Gaslight* and all that."

"And you being so, um, special..." said the Bag Lady, her voice fading under the scowl of Fanny, who was fiercely swinging.

"A three-legged sheep with a skateboard for a foot, that's who I am named after." She skidded off the swing and landed on her backside. Betty helped her up.

"You're named after a sheep," I said.

"She's exaggerating as always," Mavis whispered.

"I saw the pictures," shouted Fanny, "a great big fat ugly sheep – what the hell was he playing at?"

"There was no skateboard," whispered Mavis.

Mavis, unlike Fanny, had memories of her father.

"I hate my friggin' name," said Fanny, regaining her balance.

"I can see why," said the Bag Lady.

"He did have a sense of humour," muttered Mavis.

"The day I was born my father celebrated with a so-called *few* whiskies, then took the tractor and Fanny up the hill. He was found three days later smothered under Fanny's stomach with the skateboards lodged between..." Fanny sighed. "We won't go into that."

"That was never proven," said Mavis.

"'Call her Fanny' was scrawled on the side of the tractor – in blood. And as the sheep was still alive, Mother took it as an omen."

"I guess your name is a burden like any other," muttered Betty, who was now officially off meat.

"And that's when mother took up goat farming," muttered Fanny.

❄

Fanny stood in the kitchen dressed and ready to go. There was not a hair out of place, a whiff of alcohol, or a sign of tiredness. I offered Fanny a coffee but she refused, pulling a herbal from her bag.

"How are we this morning?" said Mavis.

"Fine." She looked at Mavis. "Any reason why not?

"You did have a few whiskies."

"It was a Gaelic hot chocolate." She looked at me. "Toast? Shall I make some?"

"Do you remember the swing?" said Mavis.

"No, why should I? I mean is there any harm in sitting on a swing?" She blushed.

"You swung upside down on it like a girl and then was sick."

"I was not."

"You were too."

"Well you brought the sloe gin, you know how that affects me," said Fanny.

"You didn't have to drink it," said Mavis.

Fanny's face went red. "Let's not talk about it." She watched Mavis flick the kettle on and picked up the only mug above the sink.

Mavis jumped. "Do you always have to take what is mine?"

"It's the only mug there, for Christ's sake," said Fanny.

"You could have asked."

"You put the kettle on – what was I supposed to do, use my hands?" snapped Fanny.

"Don't be so fucking stupid."

"Stupid? I am not the one who wrecked Mother's funeral."

Mavis sucked in her breath.

"If you hadn't put that...that show on," hissed Fanny, "and asked those stupid women..."

The Bag Lady was sitting outside. She looked up.

"It was what Mum wanted," Mavis said quietly.

Fanny, regaining her composure and waving at the Bag Lady, muttered, "Let's not talk about it."

The Bag Lady waved back.

Fanny looked at me with a sweet smile. "Would you like a herbal?"

"She drinks coffee in the morning," said Mavis.

"I only asked," snapped Fanny.

"No," I jumped in. "Mavis has made me a coffee."

Fanny's phone went off; she walked into the lounge and began to talk.

"They weren't stupid last night, were they?" Mavis muttered to me.

I patted her hand.

Fanny walked back into the kitchen. "I need to go soon," she said.

Mavis looked at her. "What about the photos?"

"Mum gave you photos?"

"Yes..."

"I thought she left them all to me."

"Well she didn't," said Mavis. "Do you want some – of Dad?"

"You're taking the piss." Then she looked at me and shook her head.

"I liked Dad," said Mavis.

"Yes, well you were old enough to know him. All I knew about him was what Mother told me, put me off men for years."

Mavis laughed. "She said you'd say that."

"What?"

"In her notes and letters and things."

"She left you letters too?"

"Yes," said Mavis.

"Oh." Fanny stared out into the garden. A tear rolled down her cheek.

"Well you got the last handing holding revelations, which you kept to your fucking self."

"Yes. Well...yes, I did that." She wiped the tear as another one fell.

Mavis handed her a paper towel. "There is a photo of you," said Mavis.

"With the goat?" Fanny looked her – her eyes welled.

Mavis nodded.

"She said she'd lost that photo." Fanny sighed. "I knew she hadn't – loved that goat."

"Then why don't you take it?" I said.

"She killed it and never told me," said Fanny. "She said the goat was lonely, and the vet had found a new home for it with other goats."

"Lots of parents say things like that," I said.

"Mother made me lead it away." She blew her nose. "To the vet's, said it was a lesson in letting go. Letting go – what a thing to say to a child. That goat trusted me, and I led it to its death. I wasn't stupid. I knew what was going to happen but had to pretend to keep Mother happy." She looked out the window. "It was very traumatic."

Mavis went to find the photo as Fanny and I stared out of the window at the Bag Lady rustling about. Fanny's face crumbled as she sipped her tea. She looked more like Mavis than ever before.

I was about to ask if she was okay when the Bag Lady began to shout about her arm being "as good as new," and "look, no bites."

"That's great," muttered Fanny with a wave.

Mavis handed her the photo.

Fanny looked at the photo for a moment with a watery smile and then stood up.

"I need to go. Thanks and sorry about the swing, although I really don't remember."

She held out her hand to Mavis, Mavis went in for an awkward hug, Fanny froze, and Mavis moved back and stiffly patted her on the shoulder.

"Better say goodbye to Herself." Fanny laughed uncomfortably and left the kitchen.

Mavis and I watched from the window as the Bag Lady handed her a painted stone and patted her on the back. Fanny drove out the drive with one arm waving as she stared ahead.

"Did you ever speak to Heather," I asked, "about your mother's last hours?"

"Yes," said Mavis, "and I thought about telling Fanny, until last night." She looked at me and sighed. "I actually felt sorry for her."

Mavis waved goodbye.

"Me too," I said. "A three-legged sheep, as if."

"That sheep was so fat," laughed Mavis, "that she toppled with just a turn of her head – took three people to help her to her feet again." Mavis started to wash the cups. "You know, I have great memories of Dad." She chuckled.

Mavis talked about a dad who let her sit on his knee while driving a tractor. Who made sloe gin in the greenhouse and fed toast dripping in butter to Fanny his pet sheep – a sheep that loitered about the back door and bleeped when the toaster pinged.

She looked at me with a childish grin.

"He made me laugh a lot. Guess I was lucky."

Chapter Forty-Two

THE REAL STORY

Yesterday's constipation, today's piles.

Mavis and Kamal walked back into the restaurant as Amanda continued on about how a sheepish-looking Mrs Campbell walked into her shop with a half-hearted "Sorry love," offering.

"Guess I shouldn't have moaned about the giro to Lumpy," she said, then plonked a couple of Mars Bars on the counter with a "Here, let's forget about the raffle" and walked out.

Lumpy had told Mrs Campbell a full church saw the assault and a raffle was the least of her worries. "If you want to go on yelling at the ex in the middle of the night, I suggest you start apologising – with chocolates – before a complaint is made."

"Can't believe it. Mrs Campbell never apologies to anyone," said Mavis.

"Aye, that Lumpy's some man," said the Roadworks Man.

"Amanda is lying," Kamal said to Mavis. Mavis eyed him. "Or maybe it's Lumpy."

"Sure miss Lumpy," said the Roadworks Man.

"She even looked a little ashamed," said Amanda. "If that's possible?"

"That woman looked ashamed when she saw me too," said Kamal.

"I was there," said Tenzam. "She yelled, and you gave her free pakoras."

Mavis looked at Kamal.

Kamal shrugged. "It's true, I gave her free pakoras."

"I offered Lumpy a book token," said Amanda, "any book he wanted, as a thank you like, and do you know what he took? *Men Are from Mars, Women Are from Venus*. It was the only copy."

Kamal left soon after that with the phone to his ear and the week's takings in a bag.

Mavis watched the door slam behind Kamal and called him a lying arsehole.

"Could have told you that," said the Roadworks Man.

"Fanny is welcome to him and his free pakoras," she said.

"Hear, here," muttered the Roadworks Man. "Not a patch on our Lumpy."

Chapter Forty-Three

THE CELEBRATION OF A LIFE

Goodbye is but a mere full stop of the sentence.

It was not long after Fanny had driven out of my drive that she began texting orders to Mavis about their mother's celebration-of-life day.

"Lumpy arranged a deal with his boss in the community centre, and Kamal offered a selection of Bangladeshi dishes in exchange for free back treatments."

Tenzam went into hysterics, claiming that she'd be doing his back for months to pay off his offer.

Mavis said nothing and went into her room. She picked up the one photo of her, her mother, Fanny, and Lumpy together and tossed it in a box.

Fanny asked Mavis if she could "do a few egg sandwiches for those who don't do curry? And perhaps some of those dips and things from the co-op?"

Fanny apparently didn't have time to organise food, what with the back treatments, auctioning her mother's jewellery, as well as organising photos of the village she was donating to. She was physically and mentally drained, as she put it, and needed all the help she could get – or, as Mavis put it, as many people as possible to boss about.

"I want pictures of the village on the wall of gratitude," she said, "the last show before they refurbish the community centre and knock the wall down. It's what *she* would've wanted."

Fanny talked a lot about what *she* would have wanted.

While Mavis kept asking, "When? When did she buy such expensive jewellery, where did she put it, and when was she interested in helping people she didn't know?" – sending Fanny into a frenzy of "You don't know her like I did – we were so close," rants.

Mavis called Fanny many things and finally, feeling charitable, came to the conclusion that Fanny was completely overcome with grief and did her best to help. Until Fanny told Mavis where she could put her suggestions.

"Nothing goes on that wall of gratitude except what I say."

Mavis, forgetting all charitable feelings, told her to get stuffed, as "the last thing her mum would have wanted was photos of a village she'd never heard of from the sale of jewellery she never wore."

They didn't speak for two days.

Instead, Mavis took to belly dancing under the stars when it was dry and inside when it was raining.

While Fanny managed to rustle up a *do* with the help of many, then look like she had done it all.

The day of celebration was a couple of hours in the afternoon between the mothers-and-toddlers group in the morning and the after-school club in the afternoon. Fanny had already covered up the wall of gratitude with a calico "Feed the World" veil when we walked in. She was standing by a table with Kamal's restaurant leaflets in a pile and three teenagers tuning their violins.

The wall of gratitude was in the middle of the community centre, a square room which led to all the other rooms and the kitchen. Everyone had to walk through, and Fanny seemed to know them all, even the mothers from the mothers-and-toddlers group who filled the centre. Fanny waved and shouted out *hello*s as a sea of children ran through the room clutching sheets of finger paintings.

Which, according to Fanny, Cat would have loved.

"This is why I didn't want to get married here," said Mavis, "it's like a circus at Asda."

"You have a point," I muttered.

Mavis stared at Fanny "holding court," as she put it. "Look at her – she's like something out of *X Factor*."

"She's worse than me," I said.

Mavis sighed. "Nothing changes with her."

Some mothers stopped to talk, others looked at the restaurant leaflets. Fanny told them all to stay, try a little curry, and celebrate the life of a woman sadly missed. "She would love it," said Fanny. She wiped her eyes. "I mean would have."

"Typical," muttered Mavis.

Fanny caught my eye and gestured to the leaflets, asking if I could "sort of scatter them about."

I, "not hearing," followed a mute Mavis into the kitchen as the teenagers began to play Neil Diamond's "Cracklin' Rosie."

Sheryl and Steven were in the kitchen helping with the food, although Sheryl looked like she would rather be anywhere than near food.

"It's the curry," she said. "The smell, I don't understand it."

"Maybe an egg sandwich will help?" I said as she raced to the toilet.

Mavis's egg sandwiches were the first to go, beating all the cream cakes and Kamal's extravagant offers – but then, that might have had something to do with Lumpy and when and where he put Kamal's curries.

Lumpy was in charge of the kitchen and beyond. He'd suggested a buffet spread over the afternoon of speeches and unveiling which Fanny had planned. And he timed the curries for after Fanny's speech, completely unaware of Fanny's timing.

So he said.

After the last of the egg sandwiches had gone and half a dozen Neil Diamond songs had been played, Fanny began the second part of her speech: a monologue that belonged in a Shakespearian play and spoken like a Shakespearian actor. It went on for three pages, in which time a crying baby was fed, watered, and changed and two rounds of drinks were handed around. It took Fanny and the rest of us through many emotions, tears, laughter, and boredom and ended with a thank-you to the carers along with a Kamal meal voucher.

"Especially you, Heather," said Fanny, handing her a tub of oil for thread veins as well as her meal voucher.

Heather looked touched as she turned the jar in her hand. "Her legs were legendary," she muttered. "Not a thread vein in sight. She said it was the lemon juice on her legs that did it." Heather let out a nervous laugh at the crowd. "Maybe there is some lemon juice in this?"

We started to clap.

"We were so close, Mother and me," continued Fanny over the clapping, "like pals." The clapping subsided. "Only she understood my need to give to the world."

Fanny pulled the veil from the wall as the teenagers began to play "Song Sung Blue," and everyone stared at the photos of an unknown African village celebrating clean water.

Mavis looked at her watch and then stared blankly ahead.

She had plans, which it seemed Fanny had forgotten.

Chapter Forty-Four

THE CRITICS

One woman's cake is another woman's baking

Mavis had spent the nights before her mother's celebration day belly dancing. Every evening she performed in front of Sheryl, the Bag Lady, and Betty, who watched, scored, and suggested improvements.

Sometimes I joined in.

Mavis practised her Zaghareet to sound like she was entertaining rather than going to war. She tried various scarves, canes, and candles for props, and the Bag Lady tried a variety of James Bond themes and Neil Diamond songs. Heather even popped around and gave belly dancing a go. It seemed like old times – like a belly dancing class.

One night I asked Amanda to join us. She was sitting in the take-away mournfully staring at her food, sending the Roadworks Man into a state of confusion. He'd spent the last hour making the usual annoying comments and gotten nothing but "a-huh," "is that right," and "if you say so" back.

He had tried everything for a reaction and in the end looked at me with a "what's up with her?" face.

"I made you something special," Tenzam said, placing a plate in front of Amanda. "Extra ghee and some cheese."

"Thanks." She feigned a smile. "I'm not hungry."

"Since when are you not hungry?" snapped the Roadworks Man. "What's wrong with you?"

"Nothing."

"Funny kinda nothing."

Tenzam turned on the TV, flicked through the Bollywood films, and stopped at Salman Khan, a Bollywood actor who had been around since the first time flared jeans were fashionable. Salman was in an extra-tight police outfit, effortlessly sprinting across the top of containers in a warehouse. His short back and sides didn't move an inch. He had a body which looked like it spent hours pumping weights, a cheesy-looking moustache, and the ability to move anything like it was made of air. His specialty was defeating a whole army of idiots with no help apart from a wry look, slow-motion camera work, and dancing. And he was in the middle of just such a scene when Tenzam flicked on the TV.

All Bollywood actors danced, but Salman Khan's was different – he wasn't sexy. His hip moves were humorous rather than erotic, and they were always accompanied with a satirical smile that would get a laugh in any *Carry On* film.

He was Amanda's pet hate.

We waited for the usual "his fighting makes American wrestling look like a documentary" comment.

Amanda stared ahead.

Salman Khan jumped from one container to another, kicking several men into a coma. Then, like a panther, he landed on the ground and swung around with a high kick, knocking a six-foot giant to the floor.

"As if," I said.

The Roadworks Man turned up the volume. The six-foot giant began to beg for mercy in Hindi.

Tenzam and the Roadworks Man looked at Amanda. She blinked, sighed, and asked for a Coke.

Salman Khan, with his foot on the giant's chest, untied a woman half his age and pulled her to him. Their lips touched.

"Men are real men in India," said the Roadworks Man with a slight spray of naan.

"Hmm," said Amanda.

"They know what's what with women."

"Uh-huh."

The Bollywood couple began to dance through the warehouse, picking up a chorus of brightly dressed dancers. They headed outside, where it started to rain, and as their clothes stuck to their bodies Salman and his woman sang, danced and cooed through a variety of costume and scenery changes.

The Roadworks Man gestured at the screen with his fork. "Bet you his wife doesn't have any complaints."

"He has no wife," muttered Amanda. "He is a playboy like that ex-husband of mine."

The Roadworks Man shifted in his seat.

"Your ex?" said Tenzam, switching off the TV just as the giant began to join in the dancing.

Amanda looked up. "He's left," she sighed. "It wasn't my furniture he left to sort but the love of his life, an old flame." She stared at her food. "Seems I was never either."

"Could have told you that," said the Roadworks Man.

She looked at me. "I've known for ages – just couldn't face it."

"Very sad," said Tenzam.

"Yes, she is a woman with her feet firmly on the ground," muttered Amanda, "not like me, apparently."

She poked at her food.

Tenzam told her she could have it on the house.

She smiled at him. "And I'm left with a bookshop, a couple of geese, and an empty house."

"Could have told you he's not coming back," said the Roadworks Man.

"Thanks for that," said Amanda.

"Could see it in his face."

"Is that right."

"Anyone could tell he'd lost interest," said the Roadworks Man.

"We get the picture," I said.

"The man's an idiot," muttered the Roadworks Man.

Amanda looked at him.

"To leave you."

Amanda gave him a weak smile.

"You're almost as much fun as Lumpy," said the Roadworks Man.

She looked at Tenzam and sighed. "It's a lot to keep up on your own."

"You need help," said the Roadworks Man.

"She knows that," said Tenzam.

"I'll need to get someone to work in the shop," said Amanda.

Tenzam gestured to me. "She doesn't work here during the day." He looked at me. "You liked working there."

"Aye that's right, you used to work there," said the Roadworks Man.

Amanda pulled a piece off the Roadworks Man's naan, dipped it in her sauce, and threw me a small smile.

Amanda was not a natural dancer; she struggled with each move. After one song she gave up, grabbed the Bag Lady's drum, and began to bang it like a three-year-old. The Bag Lady was in the teepee at the time – hunting for Mavis's music.

"Told you Betty, that drum's no toy," she shouted.

"It's not me," Betty shouted back as Mavis jumped out of the hot tub and wrapped a towel about her.

None of us heard the Bag Lady's answer as another James Bond theme tune blared from the teepee and Amanda, now lost in the moment, began to drum louder.

"Mavis, give us a dance," yelled Sheryl from the hot tub.

Mavis, with a "throw caution to the wind" stance, tossed her towel in the air and pulled a scarf about her wet hips.

"Veil or no veil?" She gestured. And before any of us had a chance to shake or nod – we'd all given up shouting – the teepee flap opened, and a veil flew out, landing at Mavis's feet. Mavis slung it about her shoulders like a vamp.

It was a dry, hot night with thick mist and a full moon, and the women had spent most of it dipping in and out of the hot tub while talking about Mavis's dance for the next day. It was still a toss-up between several James Bond theme songs. However, Neil Diamond had been given the flick the previous night, as Fanny had hogged most of his songs.

Apart from *Jonathan Livingston Seagull*.

Mavis circled her shoulders as her arms flowed to the orchestra's melody. We sat back to enjoy until she started to mime...

None of us understood it.

In fact, the women were so engrossed in trying to "get" the act that none noticed Lumpy standing in the drive – a shadow in the mist.

Fanny had asked him to "pop across" and pick up the photos for the wall she had sent to Mavis. She wanted Lumpy and Mavis to hang them up early before she got there, and for once Mavis didn't argue.

She swirled around the fire with a mischievous flair.

"These last few nights have been magic," said Mavis, "the most fun I have had in ages."

"Me too," said Amanda, now thrashing the drum, which she turned out to be as bad at as dancing.

I was beginning to wonder if she was deaf.

"Don't know why I didn't think of you," Amanda shouted to me.

"I don't know why you don't listen to the music," yelled the Bag Lady, whose head appeared from the flap of the teepee. Then with a tut she took the drum off Amanda, stating that she was "murdering the song."

Mavis was wearing a full-piece purple swimsuit which had a short 1920s fringe about her hips. The fringes shimmered with each hip flick, and once Mavis noticed, she increased her flicks with more intensity.

As the song came to an end, Mavis circled about the hot tub. She fluttered her scarf over the head of each woman, flicked it into the air, and shimmied – sending the fringes into a mesmerising series of flutters.

"Whoo-aaargh," yelled Amanda, sneaking a bang on the Bag Lady's drum.

The Bag Lady threw her a glare.

Mavis, with a superbly timed breast lift, halted with a pose and then bowed to the applause.

"What do you think?" she said. And before any of us had a chance to say:

Wonderful — nearly there.

Marvellous — not sure about the mime.

At least you've nailed the end.

Shirley Bassey's voice filled the air as she belted out:

"Goldfinger..."

Mavis's face lit up with an "I have an idea" look.

Mavis, with an exaggerated "inspired" expression, began a parody of Shirley Bassey's hand swirls, working up to a mime as cheesy as a silent film. Her hand fluttered around her face and down her body... leading into a dying swan act with her on the ground.

She lifted her head, pointed to an imaginary gold ring, then looked around, clutched at her throat, and gasped her last breath. The song finished with a blare of trumpets.

Mavis sat up. "Too stupid?"

"No more than last night's attempt," said the Bag Lady. "You've taken the whole James Bond thing too far."

"Mum loved James Bond," said Mavis.

"But not mimed, like Charlie Chaplin," said the Bag Lady.

Mavis looked at Sheryl and Betty.

"It is a bit confusing," said Sheryl.

"Why not try a different song," said Betty.

Mavis looked at me.

"Give the James Bond a rest."

"Thank God," said the Bag Lady.

"So what should I do?" said Mavis. She took her sister's stance, imitating her voice. "What would Mother want?"

"I'd go easy on the comedy," said Amanda. "Not everyone likes to laugh about dying."

Mavis slumped down on her chair. "My sister's got this whole save-the-world monologue prepared, leaving me five minutes and one song, and I have no idea what to do."

The Bag Lady, with an "I'll save the day" look, gestured for me to change the music.

I looked at her. My iPod was in her tent; was she asking me to go in?

"Go on," she said.

I stood up, made to go, and then turned back. "Me, in your tent?"

"It's your iPod," she said.

"But, *your* tent?"

"It's a teepee, not a tent."

I was stunned. All this time – all those stupid excuses.

"Betty's in the hot tub," she said.

I looked at Betty. She gestured with her glass above the bubbles and steam.

"And" – the Bag Lady gestured to Amanda – "I'm needed here to guard the drum; can't let her back on it."

I felt like a little girl being told for the first time she can go down the street and buy something important – on her own.

"Off you go; hurry up, before Shirley Bassey starts again."

I looked across at Lumpy still in the misty shadows; he threw me a wave, and I went inside the teepee.

Chapter Forty-Five

THE TEEPEE AND THE SNAKE

Ceremonies are for the living; the dying have already left.

The teepee was nothing like I had imagined. I had no set picture in my head as such, but she was a Bag Lady, and in the end, I was surprised by what I saw.

I half expected old socks, skulls, bits of junk, and a bed like Tracey Emin's. I imagined it to be damp, cold, and crammed with heaps of dirty clothes and Puss lost in the middle – somewhere.

How little I knew her.

Her teepee was warm, earthy, and large enough to hold three of Tracy Emin's beds along with all the junk beside it and a dance around the junk.

And Puss was easy to spot – stretched out on the end of a futon in one of her "how long can I make my body look" poses. She was basking in the glow of the wood stove and purring heavily when I walked in. She looked up, meowed with an "oh it's you" look, and then snuggled into a ball to continue purring.

Around the stove were orange and red cushions and blankets. And hanging from my meditation pyramid – *I always wondered where that went* – were gold and silver trinkets, small medals, and beads glistening in the light of the fire.

The floor was an old pale pink shag pile with orange and grey mats on top – *a throw away from the Argyll.* I remembered Shifty grudgingly lugging a rolled-up carpet into the garden with Betty behind him shouting how it was "cheaper than a skip."

There were a couple of familiar-looking boxes from the Read to be Thankful bookshop, now decorated with painted shells and mirrors. By the fire was a tray with a teapot – *mine* – mugs – *also from the bookshop* – and a biscuit tin – *no idea where from, but I'm sure I know where the biscuits came from.*

And leaning against the wall were two of Rodger's pictures, painted before Shifty came into his life. Which is probably why he left them behind. They were both of Puss, one dressed as a little girl and the other dressed as a priest.

I remember those pictures and at the time wondered what was going through Rodger's head. Rodger called it his cartoon phase, which lasted all of two Puss pictures and a note book full of "fuck it" scribbling across childlike drawings.

Sheryl poked her nose in. "Hurry up, the Bag Lady's getting fidgety...

I looked at the iPod, flicked through some tracks, and picked a belly dancing tribal track; "Elila Farh" by the Katir Hicham Orchestra – lots of drums, clapping, and no chance of a mime.

I could see Mavis's shadow embrace the music within one beat. Then Lumpy appeared from a hidden entrance – which I still couldn't find.

We watched Mavis's shadow effortlessly dance around the teepee as her round body painted the rhythms of the music.

She pulled scarves one at a time from her belt like a striptease as the women egged her on.

More, Mavis, give us more.

Swing it, Mavis.

If only Lumpy could see you now.

Layers of scarves were pulled from her belt and swung round her head.

Then she pulled a feather boa from somewhere and began to swing it. Soon it became an imaginary snake with a life of its own. She mimed a wrestle until it began to hypnotise her, enticing her to roll her stomach and do a few Beyoncé butt moves, which led to her miming back pain.

I watched my first student, wondering where she got her ideas from – not from me. I can't even make a baby laugh; my peekaboo sends them hiding in their mother's arms. I even scare homeless people, apart from the Bag Lady.

Mavis always had a gift for the ridiculous.

The song was coming to an end and so was the wrestling with the snake. Mavis wrestled it to the ground, came up with it tucked in her scarf, and swung it. The snake was now a penis, with a life of its own.

Lumpy laughed out loud – which made me wonder what they used to get up to when they were together.

"What are you doing in my teepee?" yelled the Bag Lady as she pulled open the flap.

Lumpy and I jumped – and then went outside.

Sheryl was sitting by the fire drinking water with a glow about her – despite feeling sick. She was waiting for Steven to pick her up. "I am not as bad as I was," she muttered.

"You're not doing that tomorrow, are you?" said Amanda. "A penis snake in the community centre?"

Mavis shook her head and talked about doing a traditional dance with a scarf that I had taught her. "It's a boring one," she said.

"Thanks," I said.

"But I can see now comedy is probably not the way to go."

"You mother will have moved on by now," said Betty. "The ceremony is for those left behind."

"When in doubt, do nothing," said the Bag Lady.

Chapter Forty-Six

VIOLINS AND NEIL DIAMOND

As long as your mother is alive, you are still a little girl wanting her approval.

In the end, Mavis didn't do any dance.

Fanny's monologue ran over the booked time of the room. Fanny didn't even get a chance to finish with the planned Neil Diamond's "I Am, I Said" on violins. While she was still basking in the applause from her monologue, the after-school club descended into the room and the celebration of Cat's life was over.

All the arguing, planning, and sandwich making – lost to a sea of dumped school bags and kids pushing and yelling.

Mavis stoically packed her things and walked to the car. I followed her out with the player; she opened the boot and looked at me.

"It's all over," she said, "a life celebrated with curry and finger painting."

"Your mother would have loved it," said a young woman pushing a pushchair past.

Mavis nodded as the woman walked away. "I doubt it," she muttered to me. "But then what would I know? The woman who wrote those notes, who Heather and Fanny talk about, I don't even know – she's a *complete* stranger. The mother I remember hated just about everything."

"You're not alone," said Heather, appearing with an armful of "save the world" photos. "I see it all the time, you'd be surprised."

Heather dumped the photos in the boot like they were bags of rubbish.

"My mother hates swearing, she even has a swear box. Then one night I went to pick her up – a *girl's night out* – and there she was leaning on the bar telling a story with the language of a porn star."

Heather eased the boot shut and looked at us.

"Not that I watch porn-like."

Mavis and I had spent an hour clearing up with Lumpy and Heather.

As the violins packed up, Fanny's son cleared the wall of gratitude while her daughter toyed with the leftover curry until we told her she could take it home.

Fanny never ventured into the kitchen; she spent her time talking to the stragglers about how massage, essential oils, and diet can cure almost everything except a broken heart.

"Yes," she said, "if you burnt a little lavender, you'd see a difference. Those screaming children over there would be putty in your hands."

The stragglers left soon after that.

Kamal arrived to pick Fanny and the leaflets up. Fanny's son stomped into the kitchen and dumped the rest of the pictures on the table.

"You'll need to take these," said the son, "no room in his car." He looked at his sister and pulled a face.

Fanny's daughter sighed, muttered "arsehole," and told us we could keep the curry.

Mavis was outside at the time. She and her sister were talking, and Mavis was smiling.

"You know," said Fanny, "it's a shame you're not getting married. I mean look at this place." She smiled at a boy; he poked his tongue out at her. "It's you to a tee, so homely."

Lumpy was walking by at the time with a stack of newspapers under his arm. He stopped mid-march and glared at Fanny. "This place is like the co-op before Christmas, who on earth would want to say their I-dos here?"

Mavis and Fanny chuckled, then laughed even louder when Kamal entered the room and tripped over a school bag.

"Mind!" shouted one schoolboy.

"Have a good trip," laughed another while the other poked out his tongue again.

Kamal dusted himself off and growled.

"Guess you're right," said Fanny. "Kamal hates this place, says it's worse than a Bangladeshi fish market."

Mavis let out another laugh, then walked into the kitchen. "We need to take the pictures home," she said. "Apparently there is no room in his lordship's car."

Mavis looked at the curry. There was a lot left.

"We should take this back for the Bag Lady and Betty, eat it by the fire, and I can show Heather how to make a feather boa turn into a boa constrictor."

She started to pack away the food. "There is loads here," she said and walked to the doorway.

"Hey, Lumpy," she shouted across the hall.

Lumpy poked his head out of the store cupboard.

"Why don't you come over and have some curry with us later?"

Lumpy, with a thumps-up, smiled.

Mavis jumped in the car. "Do you know what Fanny said to me?"

I reversed the car.

"'You didn't need to belly dance today, Lumpy had already seen you.'"

EPILOGUE

"There is never a last dance," Nefertiti

The first thing Fanny did was change her name, and Kamal was the last to know.

Cat, formerly known as Fanny, had put a small piece in the paper which the Roadworks Man read out to a surprised Kamal and an amused Amanda.

> *I, Fanny, of Fanny's Magical Hands,*
> *hereby change my name to*
> *Cat*
> *after my dear departed Mother.*

Cat no longer answered Kamal's calls. Kamal was miffed. "I only got two massages out of her," he moaned, "and one of them was a head-and-shoulders; how is that to help my back?"

Once Kamal started talking about free back treatment for his whole family, Cat changed her phone number, and the only people she gave her new number to were the Bag Lady and Betty.

Mavis laughed it off; she was busy with Lumpy. They never talked about marriage, but instead they helped with the refurbishment of the community centre and made plans for a round-the-world trip – first stop: Bangladesh.

Lumpy came around every night but never went into the hot tub. I suspect the Bag Lady and Betty practising with Mavis's feather boa was what put him off, although he blamed his legs, claiming they weren't "fit for the human eye."

Lumpy was also back in the takeaway often with Mavis, making the Roadworks Man and Tenzam happy.

In fact, Tenzam was so happy he began to try his hand at pizzas and fish and chips. Sheryl, who had gone off all thing spicy, became a regular, and when Tenzam moved on to risottos and lasagnes, she along with Mavis was never out of the place. Tenzam had developed a love for cheese and both Mavis and Sheryl were intent on introducing him to a whole new world of dairy – European style.

Tenzam's cooking was so successful he started to do the odd function. One booking was even looking for belly dancing and perhaps a little comedy.

"We could get the troupe together." Mavis's face lit up. "I could be the comedy bit. Heather would join."

"Sheryl's pregnant," I said.

"Everyone knows that," said the Roadworks Man.

"But that doesn't have to stop her. In fact, belly dancing would be great for her – I could help her."

"You sure she would want that?" said the Roadworks Man.

"Of course. Sheryl and I are thicker than clotted cream," I said.

Two months after Cat's celebration of life, Mavis was staring at the *Murder She Wrote* credits on the TV when Lumpy walked in.

Mavis handed me a tea rack. "For you," she said. "We made it, I'm fed up searching for your tea."

"I don't do tea," I said.

"You could use it as a spice rack," said Lumpy. Mavis looked at him. "Or herbs."

I looked at Mavis's bags piled at the front door. They had been packed since the morning.

"Anyone would think you couldn't wait to leave," I said.

"I not leaving; just expanding," she said and smiled. "Living with you has been a real blast."

****

Would you like to read more? Sheryl's latest adventure? Maybe Beatrice and George? Does love, sex and laughter happened after 60?

Book 4 ***Three Angry Women And A Baby*** is out now.

Please turn the page for a taster.

THREE ANGRY WOMEN AND A BABY

A stitch in time saves bugger all.

A stitch in time saves bugger all.

"I hear you're a belly dancer," said the consultant. "Been doing it long?"

"Ten years," I muttered, closing my legs.

He covered me up with a tap on my knee. "That explains it."

"What?"

"You got hips that expand like a snake's jaw," he said, laughing. "You could swallow a car."

The doctor chuckled as I glared at him with my best *is that supposed to be funny?* look. My fanny had had more viewings than a house auction with instruments that would scare a masochist, and I was supposed to enjoy a stupid joke?

"Car," I said with an angry tug at my sheet. "And what size we talking of—mini, four-wheel-drive, limo?"

The doctor flicked his gloves from his hand and tossed them in the bin. "Sense of humour, very good." He smiled, muttering something about my ability to close like a clam.

I was in the middle of a large birthing room with a door that swung open at a whisper of a wind and a foghorn-voiced doctor shouting out the size of my pelvis at a volume that I was sure even the café across the road could hear.

I glared as the consultant lathered his hands under the tap, pulled a towel from the holder, and, without looking at me, continued on about dilations and the like. The two nurses nodded while the teenage-looking students took notes. They didn't look old enough to watch a porn film, let alone handle a dilator.

According to the nurse, he—the consultant—was eccentric, and I was to take any so-called joke with a pinch of "whatever." It was one of the first things she said when I arrived, along with "get undressed," "put this on," and "we need a specimen."

"A while yet," he muttered to the older nurse.

I watched him leave, his white coat flowing like he was a caped crusader, his porn virgins following.

"Snake jaw," I said. "What sort of friggin' bedside manner is that?"

"He's Polish," said the older nurse, like somehow that explained something.

"Polish?" I muttered. "What's that got to do with parking cars?"

"He always talks about cars," muttered the younger nurse.

The older nurse smoothed down my sheet. "But he is the best. Honestly, if I were having a baby, he's the man I'd want." She looked at the younger nurse. "His episiotomies are talked about for months."

"Seamless," said the younger nurse.

I gulped. "Cuts . . . down there?"

"But don't panic." The older nurse patted my arm. "He hardly does them."

"He's more a caesarean guy, very safe," said the younger nurse.

I looked at Steven, who had just entered. "Caesarean?" I yelped. "But I did yoga and breathing."

"Honey, you have the best, he's very good. Parking cars is just his way of lightening the mood."

"Parking cars?" Steven looked at me, confused.

"Mood lightening?" I turned to Steven. "Apparently, talking about my bits like I'm a garage will have me laughing through my labour."

"It's to take your mind off things," said Steven with an *is she okay?* look at the nurse.

"Take my mind off things? That's like saying hit your head against the wall and you won't feel any pain when they cut your peri-fucking-neum."

"Let's just leave the perineum out of it," muttered Steven.

I let out a manic laugh that even I didn't recognise; my moods were seesawing all over the place.

"My mother's been going on about my perineum for months, ever since I told her I was pregnant," I joked.

Steven rolled his eyes. "She mentioned it a few times."

"'Olive oil and rubbing,' she says, 'will keep you like a virgin.'"

Steven threw a look at the older nurse. "She never said that, your mum doesn't believe in virgins."

"Steven hasn't fried anything for weeks." I laughed again and then burst into tears. "My mother's put him off olive oil for life."

Steven looked from one nurse to another, mumbling something about medication.

"Medication? That's your answer to everything," I snapped.

"Well . . . it might help, the breathing certainly isn't."

"Well, you're not trying to push out a tow truck though a pinhole, are you?" I snapped.

"Perhaps it's time for some more medication," muttered the older nurse.

Hours ago, excited, happy, and enthusiastic for a deliciously simple natural birth, I had been whipped into a labour room and given a gown the size of a napkin which hardly covered my breast.

"Is this for nose blowing?" I laughed.

The nurse, a young woman who was bustling in the corner with instruments, laughed out loud. "No dignity in this place," she said.

"It's like a doll's dress," I said, causing more giggles, until the older nurse entered.

"Having babies is no laughing matter," she said to me, "it's serious."

She eyed me, perched on a bedpan like a buoy in the water. "You done anything in that pan yet?"

I mentioned something about waiting for everyone to leave, sending a series of tuts from the older nurse.

Apparently, I had the consultant of all consultants and should be poised for inspection like a cow waiting for an insemination.

"You're lucky he's on tonight," she added before leaving.

The door swung open. I stared into the corridor, grateful it was empty. Perched on a bedpan is not something you want anyone to see.

When I discovered I was pregnant, I was so excited, so happy. Steven had bought a pregnancy test, and as we looked at the blue marker, he cried. We had wanted a baby for so long.

I prepared myself for my birth with yoga moves, belly dancing, and birth classes, rubbing oil on bits and pieces while visualising me glowing with a baby in my arms, Steven beside me, and whale music in the background.

Nothing is funny when you are having a baby. No one tells you how scared you become, how despite the whole world and its dog in the room with you, you are on your own. And no matter how many hold your hand, rub your back, and tell you "you're doing great," you are scared, petrified, that along with the baby, all your innards are going to burst out onto the table, the floor, and even the walls, and you'll never be able to shit on your own again.

When my daughter arrived, Steven punched the air like a football player, kissed me a thousand times, and then punched the air again.

I felt nothing but a huge desire to sleep and was just in the process of doing so when I felt a burning poker sear into the flesh somewhere down below.

I jolted.

My legs were spread out like a dissected frog, the consultant was playing cross-stitch with my bits below, while my daughter was being attended to under a chorus of "she's lovely," "she's beautiful," and "so like her dad."

"Keep still," snapped a male voice.

I did my best, gritting my teeth with each tug as Steven told the world and my mother that our baby girl was apparently the image of him.

"Yes, all fingers and toes," he laughed. "And Sheryl? Yes, she's fine, waiting for her tea and toast."

When it was over, I, sipping the best tea I had ever tasted in my life, cracked a joke about tapestry and how my husband would appreciate the artistic display next time he was "down there."

The consultant flicked off his gloves and moved to the sink. I was just about to sink my teeth into my toast when he, without looking up, said, "Don't I know you?"

I looked at the nurses, then Steven. *Know me?* I mouthed. *The only thing he's seen is my fanny.*

"Don't worry," said the young nurse. "He says that to all the girls."

"He's Polish," added the older nurse.

Now on sale at your favourite store
Regards and cheers

Kerrie Noor

A NOTE FROM THE AUTHOR

I hope you enjoyed Mavis's adventures inspired by my time working in my husband's Indian restaurant. Although I never actually danced in his restaurant or at a funeral I did learn how to knock up a few pakoras and the odd spicy potato...

You can find me at
www.kerrienoor.com
and like me at

facebook.com/kerrienoorwriter
x.com/kezzamac
instagram.com/kerrienoor

THANKYOUS

Editor- the lovely Sarah Kolb-Williams
Book cover designer-The wonderful libzyyy @ 99 designs
And...
To the chiefs who cooked in Ban Duic, and the Taj Mahal -my hubby's family restaurant.
I was inspired, fed and given the best seat in the house to write.
And...
of course my hubby who taught me about spices, fed me food I'd never heard off, and lots of wine when I was stuck.

ALSO BY KERRIE NOOR

Bellydancing and Beyond series :-

Book 1 :-Sheryl's Last Stand

And

Book 2:- The Downfall of a Bellydancer

Book 4- Three Angry Women And A Baby

The first three Bellydancing and Beyond books are now available on Audio (fantastic!)

Regards and cheers

Kerrie Noor

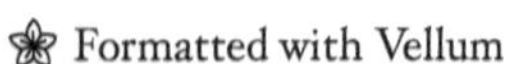 Formatted with Vellum

www.ingramcontent.com/pod-product-compliance
Lightning Source LLC
Chambersburg PA
CBHW021247200726
48288CB00015B/2696